## "Say Y[our Prayers]"

Rafe Bascomb[...]arr double action Army .44, and for a fleeting instant he actually believed he would down Preacher because the man in black hadn't moved.

Preacher had tried to reason with the boy. For reasons of his own, Preacher wasn't in a killing mood. But talk could only go so far, and theirs had petered out. As the youth went for his gun, J.D. Preacher's finely honed instincts took control. His right hand was a literal blur as it streaked to his vest holster and drew one of his forty-four forties. The boy's gun wasn't anywhere near being clear of its holster when Preacher's shot boomed in the Gold Room.

Rafe Bascomb was struck between his brown eyes, the bullet tearing through his brain and blowing out the back of his head, hat and all. Blood and flesh spattered the nearby tables and chairs as Rafe was catapulted from his feet and sent crashing into a faro bank.

# Also in the PREACHER'S LAW series:

WIDOW MAKER
TRAIL OF DEATH
THE GAVEL & THE GUN
THE LAST GUNFIGHT

# PREACHER'S LAW #5
# SLAUGHTER AT TEN SLEEP

Dean McElwain

LEISURE BOOKS  NEW YORK CITY

*Dedicated to . . .
Judy & Joshua;
and Alvin,
who won't read "nothin' but Westerns."
and
Richard O'Connor
who told it like it was.*

A LEISURE BOOK

Published by

Dorchester Publishing Co., Inc.
6 East 39th Street
New York, NY 10016

Copyright©1988 by David L. Robbins

All rights reserved. No part of this book may be reproduced or transmitted in any form or by any electronic or mechanical means, including photocopying, recording, or by any information storage and retrieval system, without the written permission of the Publisher, except where permitted by law.

Printed in the United States of America

# 1

He was going to kill the son of a bitch or die trying!

Rafe Bascomb paused in the middle of the dusty street outside of the Gold Room and pondered his next move. The way he figured it, there were two ways he could go about this. Either he waited in the dark and ambushed his man without warning, or he walked through those swinging doors and confronted Preacher face to face.

Rafe straightened, his right hand dropping to the grips on his Starr double action Army .44 strapped to his right side. The smooth texture of the polished grips reassured him. No one had ever had the gall to accuse Rafe Bascomb of being yellow, and he wasn't about to have them start now.

The streets of Cheyenne were packed with bustling people, even at this late hour. The night life of Cheyenne was in full swing; the gamblers, whores, fledgling gunmen and sundry other toughs, all hoping to make their mark. The doors to the Gold Room were seldom still. Someone was always coming or going. Part of a larger complex consisting of a hotel, a theater, a barroom, and more, the Gold Room gambling hall was frequented by high-rollers who enjoyed easy women in plush surroundings.

Rafe took a deep breath. He'd never been inside the Gold Room before. His Pa never allowed him to tote much money, and trips from Ten Sleep to Cheyenne were infrequent.

A man and a woman strolled through the doors, arm in arm, the woman laughing merrily.

Rafe moved to the doors, passing a man dressed in an expensive gray suit. He could hear more laughter, the hubbub of conversation, the clinking of glasses and the clatter of chips. Squaring his slim shoulders, he boldly entered.

Smoke filled the air. The Gold Room was crowded with customers. Many were trying their luck at the gambling tables. Painted women in tight dresses were everywhere.

Rafe walked toward the bar on the right side of the room, scanning the crowd for the man he wanted.

A brunette in a blue dress, her hair piled on her head, swayed up to Rafe. "Howdy, stranger. Care to buy a girl a drink?"

Rafe, engrossed in his search, motioned for her to move aside.

"What's wrong, honey?" she demanded sarcastically. "Don't you like what you see?"

Rafe, annoyed, stared at the whore. "Maybe later."

The brunette reached out and playfully stroked his right cheek. "Fine, lover. I'll be here." She ambled off.

Rafe reached the fancy mahogany bar and placed his back against it as he continued looking.

"What'll you have, mister?" asked a burly barkeep.

Rafe glanced over his right shoulder, about to order a whiskey, when he spotted the man he was looking for on the far side of the room, involved in a card game with four other men.

"What'll it be, mister?" the bartender asked again.

Rafe shook his head and ambled through the press of people, his brown eyes never leaving his quarry. The man he wanted was seated with his broad back to the far wall.

Someone accidentally jostled Rafe, and he angrily shoved the man aside, his total concentration on the man in black.

The man called Preacher wore a black broadcloth frock coat and a matching vest. He also wore black britches with a thin gray stripe running down the sides. By contrast, a white shirt covered his chest. His collar was secured by a black string tie. A broad-brimmed, shallow topped black hat crowned his thick, dark hair. If Preacher was heeled, his guns were hidden by his clothing.

Rafe considered, and promptly discarded, the notion that Preacher might be unarmed. He stepped past a faro bank and was now only ten yards from the table where Preacher sat, absorbed in his card game.

A lovely blonde in a red dress, her ample cleavage spilling over the top, sashayed up to Preacher, on his right side, and said a few words to him. Preacher nodded.

Rafe could feel his blood racing. He wiped his sweaty palms on his brown pants, mustering his nerve.

The blonde placed her hand on Preacher's shoulder.

Rafe clenched and unclenched his right hand a few times, flexing his muscles, limbering his hand for the draw. No one, as yet, was paying any attention to him. But that all abruptly changed when he took a step toward and shouted his challenge. "Preacher! On your feet!"

Instant pandemonium. Men and women hastened to remove themselves from the line of fire. There was muttering and curses. The four men at Preacher's table rose and collectively hurried to the left.

"Did you hear me, Preacher?" Rafe bellowed arrogantly.

The man known as Preacher sighed and looked up, his dark eyes partially obscured by his hat brim. A sweeping handlebar moustache rimmed his upper lip and both sides of his right mouth. "They could hear you in Denver, boy," he said in a low voice.

"Don't call me boy!" Rafe snapped, flustered, edgy. "You don't look to be much older than me!"

The blonde in the red dress whispered something to Preacher, and he shook his head. She calmly moved away from the table.

"Stand up!" Rafe barked.

Preacher didn't move.

"I said, stand up!" Rafe ordered nervously.

"I don't need to stand up to kill you," Preacher said quietly.

Rafe snickered. He'd never felt so alive in all his life! "You got it wrong, Preacher! I aim to kill you!"

Preacher's hands were lying on the table near a pile of chips. His hard gaze raked Rafe from head to toe. "Why?"

"Don't you know?"

J.D. Preacher studied the youth, puzzled. He pegged the

boy at fifteen, not more than sixteen years of age. What was it this time, he wondered? A wet-nosed kid out to make a rep for himself?

Preacher surveyed the boy's crumpled Stetson, his sandy hair and freckled face, his homespun shirt and pants, and knew he'd never seen the kid before. "No," he replied.

Rafe snorted. "The great Preacher can't figure it out for hisself?" He paused, his confidence bolstered by Preacher's inactivity. "I couldn't believe it when I heard you was in town! The big man with an iron! How many has it been? Near forty, I heard tell. Well, you don't scare me none, Preacher!"

Preacher was calculating the distance between them. He knew the kid would talk his ear off before making a play. His kind always did. They had more wind than gumption.

"Wait'll Pa hears about this!" Rafe was gloating. "I'll be the biggest man in Ten Sleep!"

"But will you live to tell it?" Preacher remarked.

Rafe glared at the tall man in black. "Draw, Preacher! I'm ready for ya'!"

Preacher stalled, hoping the law would arrive and intervene. He'd enjoyed a peaceful six weeks since arriving in Cheyenne and the last thing he wanted was to attract attention to himself.

"If you don't pull your iron," Rafe warned, "I'll shoot you just the same."

Preacher eased back in his chair. "What's your name?"

"Rafe Bascomb!" Rafe stated proudly.

"Should that mean something to me?" Preacher asked.

"You kilt my uncle!" Rafe exlaimed.

Bascomb? Bascomb? Preacher racked his brain, but for the life of him he couldn't recall gunning any Bascomb. "You're mistaken," he said.

"Am not!" Rafe countered belligerently. "Pa told us all about it! You shot Uncle Andy in the back! You're nothin' but a low down, rotten bushwacker!"

Preacher sensed Rafe Bascomb was preparing to reach. Although Bascomb didn't know it, Preacher was armed to the teeth. His hardware included a pair of matched, ivory gripped, customized forty-four forties, one in a vest holster under his left arm, the other on his right hip. Both guns had been specifically crafted for Preacher by a master gunsmith in Denver. Both were nickel plated, both sported barrels five and a half inches in length, and neither had a front sight. The bents were critically adjusted, giving each weapon a lightning hair trigger. Preacher also carried a Bowie knife in a sheath dangling from his belt in the center of his back. This knife bore sentimental value; it had been a gift from J.D.'s father, Dan, and was constructed of the finest quality steel. The big blade was adorned with ivory grips inlaid with silver, with Preacher's initials.

In addition to his usual armament, Preacher was carrying a recently acquired hideout. Known as a Barnes .50 boot pistol, it was loaded with only one heavy ball. Preacher had obtained the gun in a card game when a gambler foolishly got in over his head and was forced to stake part of his bet on ownership of the gun. The gambler lost. Now Preacher carried it in his right boot.

Preacher saw a wild look in Rafe Bascomb's eyes, and he tried one last time to fend off the inevitable. "Your Pa is mistaken, Bascomb. I never shot your Uncle Andy. Why don't you bring your Pa here and I'll talk to him personal like and get this straightened out?"

Rafe laughed. "It won't work, Preacher! You won't be talkin' your way out of this! Pa is in Ten Sleep."

"Why don't you go fetch him?" Preacher advised. "You shouldn't be here alone."

Rafe grinned maliciously. "Bascombs never do nothin' alone! Now say your prayers!" His right hand swooped to his Starr double action Army .44, and for a fleeting instant he actually believed he would down Preacher because the man in black hadn't moved.

Preacher had tried to reason with the boy. For reasons of his own, Preacher wasn't in a killing mood. But talk could only go so far, and theirs had petered out. As the youth went for his gun, J.D. Preacher's finely honed instincts took control. His right hand was a literal blur as it streaked to his vest holster and drew one of his forty-four forties. The boy's gun wasn't anywhere near being clear of its holster when Preacher's shot boomed in the Gold Room.

Rafe Bascomb was struck between his brown eyes, the bullet tearing through his brain and blowing out the back of his head, hat and all. Blood and flesh spattered the nearby tables and chairs as Rafe was catapulted from his feet and sent crashing into a faro bank.

Silence descended on the Gold Room. Everyone seemed reluctant to move, let alone speak. They could scarcely credit the testimony of their eyes. Some were ready to swear they hadn't seen Preacher's hand move.

The blonde in the red dress broke the spell. "Will some of you boys clean up this mess?" she called out.

Preacher replaced the spent cartridge in his vest gun and returned it to its holster.

There was a commotion from the vicinity of the doorway, and a tall man wearing a brown hat, vest, and pants, waded through the throng. A remington New Model Army .44 was strapped on his left hip, butt forward. A tin star gleamed on his vest. Clayton Landry, Cheyenne's tough-as-nails marshal, had arrived. Landry boldly strode to the fallen Bascomb and glanced at the body. He shifted his stance and glared at the man in black. "This your handiwork, mister?"

Preacher nodded, his eyes hidden by his hat.

"It wasn't his fault, Clay," the blonde chimed in. "That kid marched in here and pulled on him."

"Self defense!" hollered a hefty gambler. "Pure and simple!"

Landry frowned, his blue eyes narrowing. "What's your name, mister?"

"Preacher," came the soft reply. "J.D. Preacher."

Clayton Landry tensed. "You the one the newspapers and such been callin' the Widow Maker?"

Preacher nodded.

"The bounty hunter?"

Again, Preacher nodded.

"I didn't know you were in my town," Landry stated.

Preacher looked up, into the marshal's eyes. "I didn't know Cheyenne was *your* town."

"Where the law is concerned, mister, Cheyenne is my town," Landry said crisply. "And I don't like cheap gunmen. . . ." He suddenly stopped.

J.D. Preacher was on his feet, his right hand draped near his hip holster. "Be careful, marshal. Be real careful. I'm a mite particular about what I'm called. I didn't ask for this trouble, but I won't be prodded by any man."

Landry took a step forward, obviously angered by the bounty hunter's warning.

# SLAUGHTER AT TEN SLEEP

Another showdown loomed.

Laughing lightly, the blonde quickly moved between the two men. "What are you two trying to do? You're holding up the festivities!" She raised her pleasant voice. "Let's have a round on the house!"

The ice melted. People began talking again, milling about, returning to whatever they were doing before the gunfight erupted. With one notable exception. Everyone—*everyone*—gave Preacher's table a wide berth. Except for Clayton Landry. He stalked up to it and leaned his hands on the edge.

The blonde closed in. "Now, Clay!" she remonstrated with the marshal. "I don't want no trouble!"

"Stay out of this, Lacy!" Landry snapped. He gazed at Preacher. "I don't like being prodded any more than you do! But I'll let it drop this time because you didn't start it."

"Clay—"Lacy began.

Landry ignored her. "This is 1869, mister, not 1850. Cheyenne is gettin' civilized. Ever since the Union Pacific pushed into here from Julesburg, we've been growin' and a growin'. We're a city now, Preacher, and we can't afford gunplay. A man with your reputation attracts trouble like shit attracts flies! I want you out of my town."

"When I'm ready," Preacher responded cooly.

"You're ready when I say you're ready!" Landry threatened.

"Clay! Leave him alone!" Lacy protested.

The marshal glanced at the voluptuous woman beside him. "You and him, huh, Lacy? Well, Miss Pettibrew, who you hang out with is your affair, not mine. But don't butt into my business."

Preacher slowly moved around the table.

"Where the hell are you goin'?" Landry demanded.

"To my room."

"I'm not finished with you yet," Landry said.

Preacher turned, standing a foot from the marshal. His next words were spoken so low only Landry and Lacy heard them. "Yes, you are. And if you press me again, I'll kill you." He nodded at Lacy Pettibrew and walked away.

Landry started to go after him.

Lacy grabbed the marshal's brawny arm, restraining him. "Clay, wait!"

"What did I just tell you?" Landry retorted.

"Leave him be," Lacy said. "Don't push him. He's been going out of his way to avoid causing any grief."

"I don't care," Landry brusquely declared.

"Didn't you hear what happened?" Lacy asked.

"I've been on the road transportin' prisoners for five days," Landry said. "Rode in an hour ago, and look at what I find!"

"It was in all the papers," Lacy revealed. "How he gunned his own brother."

"Preacher?"

Lacy nodded. "His kin went bad, and Preacher went after him. Caught up with him in a place called Empire, Colorado. The Rocky Mountain News said he killed ten men, including his own brother."

"Ten men?" Landry stared at the swinging doors. "Damn!"

"I figure he came here to get away from things," Lacy speculated. "To get lost in a crowd. You see?"

"I see," Landry acknowledged. "But it don't change things none. No rotten bounty hunter gets special treatment from me." He moved toward Rafe Bascomb's body.

"You're a real sweet gent, Clay Landry," Lacy muttered under her breath.

# 2

Elizabeth Cole Demming was delighted. Her father, General Nels Demming, was hosting a formal dance in honor of their assignment at Fort Laramie. And Elizabeth loved to dance. Unfortunately for her, the opportunities to enjoy dancing had been few and far between over the years.

For seventeen years, Elizabeth had followed her father from post to post, the proverbial army brat. Before Fort Laramie, General Demming had been involved in the fiasco at Fort Phil Kearny. This fort, situated near the Bighorn Mountains, had been hated by the Sioux. They had vowed to destroy it, and in a sense the Sioux had succeeded.

Red Cloud, their most celebrated leader, a member of the Snake family, a man credited with 80 coups, had surrounded Fort Phil Kearny with some two-thousand braves. It became almost impossible to leave or enter the fort. Eighty one men under the command of Captain W.J. Fetterman were wiped out. During the first six months of the Circle of Death, as it became known, about 150 men were killed.

The army eventually agreed to give up the fort, and a treaty was signed at Fort Laramie on November 6, 1868. After the terrible tension and frightful uncertainty of Fort Phil Kearny, Elizabeth was happy to have her father posted at a relatively quiet fort where skirmishes with the Indians were rarely reported.

Now, as she hurried from their frame house to the building being used for the dance, she alternately whistled and hummed, looking forward to dancing with at least ten or fifteen of the fort's eligible junior officers. She decided to take a shortcut to assure her arriving on time. So instead of sticking to the streets, she opted to swing across a vacant lot. A full moon was overhead, illuminating the lot. She waded through waist high grass, contented and reflecting on the article she had read in the Rocky Mountain News only an hour before.

Women were going to be accorded the right to vote! Elizabeth could hardly believe it! According to the newspaper, there was a move afoot in the Wyoming territorial legislature to give women the right to vote and hold elective office. Only the year previous, the U.S. Congress had created the Territory of Wyoming, and now the territorial legislature was stirring up a hornet's nest of controversy by proposing to grant women the vote. No other territory or state had ever passed such a law. Some snobbish Easterners were claiming the members of the Wyoming territorial legislature must have cow dung for brains.

Elizabeth was halfway across the lot when she heard a twig snap to her left. She paused, surveying the grass. What had it been, she wondered? Probably a varmint of some sort. She skirted a dead tree and angled for the street.

The grass to her right unexpectedly rustled, as if a large body was weaving through the field. Startled, Elizabeth scanned the lot again. Perhaps it was a dog or a cat. Or even someone playing a prank on her. She resumed her whistling, walking faster, holding her bag in her hands.

Something crunched to the left.

Elizabeth turned, searching for some sign of whatever made the noise, and as she did footsteps pounded behind her. Before she could cry out, a heavy blanket was forcibly draped over her body, over her shoulder length black hair and her frilly white dress.

Stout arms encircled her around the waist.

Elizabeth's initial shock gave way to a burning resentment. She struggled, kicking and shouting, her voice muffled by the blanket.

Someone smacked her on the back of the head. "Quiet

down in there!" a harsh voice demanded. "Or we'll gut you right here!"

Elizabeth ceased resisting. She could tell the speaker meant business.

"Be good, ma'am, and you won't be harmed," whispered another man. "I promise."

"Well, aren't you the dandy!" joked a third.

Elizabeth was grabbed by her shoulders and ankles and swiftly transported across the field. She sensed they were heading to the west, retracing her path. Her captors abruptly stopped, and a moment later she was swung up onto a flat surface. Pain racked her knees.

"Move out!" someone barked.

Elizabeth could hear the clatter of wagon wheels and the clomp of hooves as she was borne into the night. She felt more blankets being piled on top of her. Surprisingly, instead of feeling scared, she was mad. More than mad! She was furious at her abductors for spoiling her fun, for ruining her chance to dance the night away. In addition to her exceptional beauty, Elizabeth Cole Demming was noted for one other attribute: her fiery temper. Now, as the wagon negotiated a sharp turn to the left, her temper came in handy. Her incensed state of mind prevented her from fully appreciating the gravity of her predicament.

If her captors had expected to find a hysterical woman on their hands, they were doomed to disappointment. Elizabeth even smiled as she contemplated her revenge. It wasn't for nothing she was known as Demming's Little Hellcat, as one colonel had put it.

Yes, sir! Elizabeth vowed. The sparks were going to fly!

# 3

Lacy was waiting for him in his room at the Braden House, seated on his bed, when the man in black returned.

Preacher paused in the doorway, eyeing her speculatively.

"Where you been?" Lacy asked. "I was worried."

"Went for a walk," Preacher responded. He closed the door and crossed to the dresser.

"It's nearly morning," Lacy observed, glancing at the window. "I thought maybe you weren't coming back."

"I'm here," Preacher said. He placed his hat on the dresser and moved to the washbowl on the wooden stand by the bed.

"Clay won't leave it be," Lacy remarked, watching him.

"I know," Preacher replied. He splashed a handful of cool water on his face.

"Could come to a showdown," Lacy commented.

"I reckon," Preacher said, straightening. He toweled his face, carefully whiping his moustache, and faced her.

Lacy detected the hungry gleam in his brooding eyes. She grinned. "I just came here to talk."

"Sure."

Lacy held up her left hand. It contained a bottle of Preacher's favorite drink, Teton Jack. The label depicted a mountain man straddling a dead grizzly bear. Above the caption it read: It will tame the grizzly in you!

# SLAUGHTER AT TEN SLEEP

"Brought you a gift," Lacy stated.

Preacher moved closer.

Lacy extended her arm. "Here. You look thirsty."

Preacher nodded. "I am. But not for that." He eased onto the soft bed and took her in his muscular arms.

Lacy smirked. "My momma warned me about men like you."

Preacher mustered a grin. "She was right."

Lacy kissed him passionately as his hands roved over her body. She wanted him, wanted him even more than the first time, when she had spotted him in the Gold Room just two days ago.

She'd asked the barkeep, Henry, if he knew the lanky stranger, and Henry had whispered there was a rumor going around that the man in black was the infamous J.D. Preacher. Killer! Shootist supreme! A personal friend of Wild Bill Hickock, the most famous of all the Pistoleers.

Lacy was attracted to deadly men. She could pick them out of a crowded toom with the same ease other whores displayed in latching onto rich customers. There was something about the deadly ones, about the gunmen, Lacy responded to with ardor. Their mere touch galvanized her body, aroused her to a fever pitch.

Now, as Preacher lowered her naked body to the bed, having discarded her clothes with a practiced ease, she thrilled as his fingers traced a gentle path between her legs, stroking her yielding thighs, and probed her nether lips. Vibrant sensations pulsed through her, and she spread her legs to accommodate him.

Preacher tongued her taut nipples and kneaded her pliant breasts.

She writhed and moaned, whispering "I want you!"

Preacher hastily stripped off his frock coat, shirt, and tie, and tossed them aside at the foot of the bed. He carefully placed the forty-four forties on the carpeted floor, then slid his boots beside them.

"Hurry!" Lacy goaded him, her hands massaging her nipples.

Preacher unhitched his britches and they dropped to his knees. He saw the raw lust lighting Lacy's smoldering eyes, and he didn't bother removing his pants. He settled on her, licking her neck and breasts.

Lacy squirmed and raked his back with her red nails.

Preacher drifted lower over her body, kissing and stroking her soft creamy flesh. He sank below her legs.

Lacy gasped and cooed, wriggling her bottom, delirious with passion. A sexual inferno flamed between her thighs, and she yearned to feel Preacher's huge organ inside her. "Now!" she prompted. "Please, Preacher, now!"

Preacher needed the release as much as Lacy. More, even. He drew back, aligned his organ, and plugged into her moist box. She clasped him tightly, nibbling on his left ear. Preacher moved rhythmically, his friction incensing both of them.

"Oh!" Lacy cried. "Yes! Yes! Do it!"

Preacher did. He brought her to a shuddering climax, then joined her, his lean form quivering, his muscles tight. They were breathing heavily when he finally rolled aside onto his back, near the edge of the bed. His left arm dangled over the side, hovering near his boots.

Lacy cuddled next to Preacher, her warm arm on his stomach and closed her eyes. "Nice," she mumbled dreamily.

Preacher inhaled the fragrant scent of her blonde hair. He wanted to sleep too, but his troubled mind wouldn't permit it.

He'd spent hours walking the streets of Cheyenne, lost in the crowds, savoring a temporary anonymity. Hordes of people thronged the streets, even at night. Most of them were en route elsewhere. Cheyenne was a commercial and travel hub, providing a stopping point for those headed for the Montana and Dakota Territory, despite the ever present danger of Indian attacks. Freighting outfits were making Cheyenne their terminal for merchandise. Cheyenne was booming, and some said it might one day rival Denver.

Preacher thought of Rafe Bascomb, and then of his brother. March 5, 1869 was a date he'd never forget. The day he'd gunned his own kin. True, Zachary Daniel Preacher, his older brother and only remaining relative, had gone bad. But Preacher wished there might have been another way. After all, they'd both lost their parents, Daniel and Matilda Preacher, to murdering carpetbaggers. The army claimed Zack had led the attack on Bradburn Hill, the Preacher plantation. But had he? Preacher suddenly realized he hadn't bothered to ask Zack the truth. He'd simply taken the army's assertion for granted.

Was it mere coincidence that the bastards had next ravaged Langhorne Oaks, and estate only eight miles from Bradburn Hill, and the home of the woman Preacher had loved, Rosamond Langehorn? Why had the carpetbaggers killed everyone at both plantations, except for Rosamond and Abigail, Preacher's sister? Strangest of all, why had Rosamond and Abigail later traveled west and wound up with Zack in Empire, Colorado? None of it added up, and Preacher wished he had the answers.

Preacher remembered the last words Zack had spoken. "Happy birthday, little brother."

Happy birthday! Preacher had killed Zack the day before his twenty-third birthday. He recollected those final moments with horrible clarity. Zack pulling his gun, and he was fast, so fast. Zack's hasty shot missed though, shattering a glass on the bar in front of Preacher. Before Zack could fire again, Preacher shot him twice, once between Zack's eyes, the second through Zack's heart. Zachary Daniel Preacher died with a blank expression on his face.

Lacy shifted in her sleep.

Preacher had believed he didn't give a damn about Zack. Now, he knew he'd been wrong. He sighed. The past was past, and there was no sense in troubling himself about it. He had to face the future.

What were his prospects? He liked bounty hunting. The job fit him like a leather glove. But he was fast growing tired of the notoriety attached to the profession. Those damned newshounds were everywhere, and every gunfight he was involved in became fuel for their literary fire. The yellow journalists embellished the tales, turning them into epic adventures of derring-do, replete with maidens in distress and vile villains. They also extolled Preacher's gun handling to the point where any aspiring gunny in the territory was ready to risk his life in the attempt to gain immortal fame by killing the legendary shootist, J.D. Preacher.

Preacher frowned. He didn't like the fame he'd acquired. He didn't like constantly being challenged by wet-nursed kids like Rafe Bascomb.

Rafe Bascomb. The youth had insisted Preacher shot his kin. Uncle Andy. Andy Bascomb? Andrew Bascomb? The name jarred Preacher's memory, but he couldn't place it for certain. Where had Rafe Bascomb called home? Ten Sleep? Wasn't that it? Preacher had never been to Ten Sleep, a tiny town in the north-central part of the Wyoming Territory. He wondered if there were more Bascombs living in Ten Sleep, and if they would show up to avenge Rafe.

Preacher was starting to doze off. His eyelids closed once, twice, and as he opened them for the third time he imagined he was dreaming, because walking into the room was the ghost of Rafe Bascomb. No doubt about it. The same sandy hair. The same brown eyes. The same freckled face. But something was wrong here. The ghost was wearing new homespun clothes, a blue shirt and pants, and it wore a floppy black hat while Rafe had worn a Stetson. And instead of holding a Starr double action Army .44, the ghost had a Model 1860 Army Colt .44 caliber revolver. In the ghost's left hand was a room key. On its face, a wide smirk.

"Well, lookee here! The high and mighty Widow Maker caught with his britches down! Too bad Rafe can't see this!"

Preacher was instantly awake. This wasn't a dream! It was for real!

Lacy snored away on his chest.

"Are you scared, Widow Maker?"

Preacher's left hand touched the top of his right boot.

"You should be, *hombre*! Say your prayers!" the youth taunted Preacher.

Preacher went to sit up.

"Don't even think it!" the boy warned, his voice rising. "I ought to shoot you right now, but I want you to know who I am before I pull this trigger!"

"You're another Bascomb," Preacher deduced, his left hand inching into his right boot.

"That's right, Widow Maker! Rufus Bascomb! You done kilt my twin last night!"

"Any more of you Bascombs around?" Preacher asked.

"A passel of 'em," Rufus boasted. "Why?"

"Just wanted to know if any of your kin would be coming for me after—" Preacher said.

Rufus Bascomb appeared puzzled. "After what?"

"After I kill you." Preacher's left hand swept the Barnes .50 caliber from his right boot, the heavy gun thundering in the confines of the room.

Rufus Bascomb was hit in the forehead, the bullet splattering his brains over the door as he was flung backward, arms outstretched, through the doorway and into the hall. He crashed against the far wall, then slumped to the floor, trailing a red swath on the wall.

Lacy, startled from her slumber, jumped up. "What?" she blurted sleepily.

Preacher shoved her from him. "Get dressed," he ordered. He donned his clothes, moving quickly, leaving the hideout on the bed as he replaced his prized forty-four forties in their respective holsters.

Voices sounded in the hallway. "Get the marshal!" someone yelled.

"What'd I miss?" Lacy asked, buttoning her red dress.

"Rufus Bascomb," Preacher responded succinctly. He crossed to the dresser and retrieved his hat.

"Another Bascomb?" Lacy stated. "They're worse than rabbits!"

Preacher walked into the hallway. Men and women were standing at both ends of the corridor, but none dared to venture nearer.

"It's the Widow Maker!" someone exclaimed.

Preacher knelt and rifled Rufus Bascomb's pockets. He found four dollars and another fifty cents in small change, some matches, and a small pocket knife, all in Bascomb's pants. He reached into Bascomb's shirt pocket and found a piece of paper. He returned to his room and unfolded it, discovering a faded newspaper clipping. It was from the Bloomfield Vindicator.

## THE WIDOW MAKER

### Assassin or Avenger

The town of Bloomfield is astir today with the news of a gunfight on our main street. One of Bloomfield's prominent citizens, Andrew Bascomb Posey, was shot by an unidentified assailant in broad daylight. Posey has been the subject of much controversy recently because of claims he once rode with the infamous William Quantrill. Posey had denied he was with

Quantrill during the savage raid on Lawrence, Kansas. The Army reportedly wanted to question Posey about two raids on private homes in Tennessee, where families at Bradburn Hill and Langhorne Oaks were virtually wiped out. Another alleged participant, Jesse Meeks of Muhlenberg County, Kentucky, was killed by an unidentified man in black last October. Now Andrew Posey has been gunned down here in Missouri. This paper believes there is a connection between the two deaths. Both Meeks and Posey allegedly rode with Quantrill; both allegedly conducted raids in Tennessee; both have been killed by a mysterious man in black; both have left widows in their wake. Who is this Widow Maker? Is he an avenger or a dastardly assassin? What are his motives? The Army is interested in the matter, and details will be forthcoming shortly.

Preacher lowered the paper. Posey and Meeks had been part of the raiding party responsible for slaying his parents. He'd given them their chance, then killed them. What connection was there between Rafe and Rufus Bascomb and Posey? He glanced at the article once more. Andrew *Bascomb* Posey. Bascomb. Bascomb. Was there a link?

Boots pounded in the hallway.

Preacher slid the newspaper account into his coat pocket.

Marshal Clay Landry appeared in the doorway. He gazed at the body, then at Preacher. "I warned you, Preacher."

Lacy stepped forward. "We was minding our own business, Clay." She nodded at the corpse. "He came after Preacher."

"I know," Landry admitted. "The front desk clerk was pistol whipped, and the master key was stolen. I found the clerk downstairs. He'll live." He looked at the body again. "Who was he?"

"Rufus Bascomb," Preacher stated.

Landry's brow furrowed. "Rufus Bascomb? I found papers on the other one you gunned identifyin' him as Rafe Bascomb. They're not from around these parts."

## SLAUGHTER AT TEN SLEEP

"They're from Ten Sleep," Preacher said.

"How would you know that?" Landry demanded.

"Rafe told me," Preacher revealed.

"Why are they gunnin' for you?" Landry wanted to know.

Preacher shrugged. "I don't rightly know. But I aim to find out."

"You're leavin' Cheyenne?" Landry asked hopefully.

Preacher nodded.

Lacy frowned.

Clay Landry smiled. "Best news I've heard all day. I can't be wastin' time with you, not with keepin' an eye peeled for the kidnappers and all."

"Kidnappers?" Lacy repeated.

"Yup. Last night. Some yahoos kidnapped the daughter of General Nels Demming over in Fort Laramie. Took her right off the street. The whole country is in an uproar," Landry said.

"Why'd anybody want to kidnap her?" Lacy inquired.

"How should I know?" Landry retorted. "General Demming isn't a rich man. Makes no sense. But whoever did it won't get far. Posses are out all over the place. We don't cotton to having our womenfolk abducted."

He glanced at the man in black. "And we don't cotton to bounty hunters, either."

"Don't push it," Preacher said in a low tone.

Landry considered for a moment, then decided against pressing the issue. "Makes no nevermind to me, Preacher. Just so you're leavin' Cheyenne. If you're lookin' for bounty, there's a five thousand dollar reward posted for the kidnappers of General Demming's daughter."

"That's a hefty sum," Preacher acknowledged.

"Like I said," Landry declared, "We get riled when someone mistreats our women. The sons of bitches will swing. Count on it."

The marshal stared at Rufus Bascomb, frowning. "Eb Calloway, the undertaker, is gettin' rich off you, Preacher. He's chargin' folks to see Rafe Bascomb's body. See the man killed by the Widow Maker! I reckon he'll be chargin' double now."

Clay Landry departed.

Lacy turned toward Preacher. "You really leaving?"

Preacher nodded, moving to the dresser. He started to

collect his possibles.

"Ten Sleep?" Lacy asked.

Preacher nodded.

"Can't you let it lie?" Lacy queried.

Preacher glanced at her for a moment, then resumed packing his black bag.

"Stupid question, huh?" Lacy said. "What do you expect to find there?"

"Answers," Preacher replied.

"Will you be back this way?" Lacy asked hopefully.

Preacher averted her silently pleading eyes. "Never can tell," he said.

"I've heard that before," Lacy said quietly. She moved to the window and watched the brightening dawn.

# 4

Elizabeth Cole Demming lost track of the hours spent bouncing on the hard bed of the wagon. Night passed. Day arrived. The heat became oppressive, stifling, threatening to suffocate her. She took the discomfort for as long as she could, then she opened her mouth and shouted, "Let me out of here!"

"Quiet, girl!" a gruff voice responded.

"Let me out!" Elizabeth insisted angrily. "I can hardly breathe!"

"Whoa there!" another male voice shouted. "Whoa there!"

Elizabeth felt the wagon lurch to a stop. There was a swishing sound, and suddenly brilliant sunlight and fresh air washed over her. The sunlight caused her to squint as her eyes adjusted, the shimmering sunshine smarting her eyes after the dark, cramped confines of the heavy blanket.

"It's 'bout time!" she snapped.

There were four of them, all wearing homespun clothes, all armed, all hard cases. One was driving the flatbed wagon, handling the four horse team. He was youngish, with blond hair and blue eyes, wearing a brown shirt and pants and a wide brimmed hat. To the left of the wagon, astride a brown mare, was a big man wearing a black hat, black vest, and a gray shirt and black pants. His face was hawkish, almost mean, and he sported a brown moustache. On the right side of the flatbed, riding a black stallion, was the tallest of the quartet. He wore buckskins, both leggings and shirt, and a brown hat with a short brim. Seated in the wagon near Elizabeth was the last man, the one with the gruff voice, a bear of a man with a portly girth, a greasy red shirt and black trousers, and a ragged black hat with a hole in the crown. A bullet hole.

"I didn't say to stop," the man next to her said, addressing the driver.

"We can't let her smother," replied the driver. "Pa wouldn't like for us to fetch her home dead."

Elizabeth swept a strand of her hair from her angular face and glared at them. "If you scoundrels know what is good for you, you will take me to my papa this instant!"

The one with the greasy shirt chuckled. "Hush, missy. You ain't hardly in a position to demand nothin'."

"You're marked for the gallows! You know that, don't you?" Elizabeth declared.

The one near her grinned. "Don't know nothin' of the sort, missy."

"Stop calling me missy!" Elizabeth remarked.

"What should we call you?" responded the bear of a man. "How 'bout Your Highness!"

The quartet burst into laughter.

Elizabeth noticed the young driver laughed the least. She smiled at him, and the youth actually blushed.

"My papa will have the entire U.S. Army looking for me. You won't get away!"

The man with the gruff voice swept his right arm in an arc. "We've done made our getaway, missy."

Elizabeth scanned the countryside, alarmed to discover only the sweeping prairie, the rolling sagebrush and the bleached earth, with a high ridge visible off to the west. Nary a sign of habitation.

"Where are we?" she asked.

The greasy one guffawed. "Wouldn't you like to know!"

The buckskin clad rider and the mean one joined in the mirth.

"Why'd you abduct me?" Elizabeth demanded. "For ransom?"

All four men laughed.

# SLAUGHTER AT TEN SLEEP

Elizabeth scowled at each of them. "My papa will make you vermin pay for this humiliating treatment!"

"He'll pay, alright," said the man in buckskins.

More merriment.

The bearlike man leaned forward. "Listen up, missy. Pay attention. If you don't do exactly like we say, your papa will get you back in pieces. Savvy?"

Elizabeth started to speak, but thought better of the idea.

"Good," the man said. "Now here's the way it is. We've got a heap of travelin' to do. You behave the whole trip, and you'll live to see your old man again. If you don't . . ." He paused and ran his right index finger across his throat. "You savvy?"

Elizabeth reluctantly nodded.

"We're makin' progress," the man quipped. "You just keep in mind you're to do everything we tell you, when we tell you." He pointed at the driver. "That there is Burt." He swiveled his arm in the direction of the man in buckskins. "That there is Boone." Next he pointed at the rider with the hawkish features. "Him, he's Cy. Don't trifle with Cy, missy, or he'll kill you dead."

The man named Cy grinned, exposing a gap where his two top front teeth had once been.

"I'm Port," the bearlike man concluded. "We're all right pleased to make your acquaintance!"

All four snickered.

"My pleasure," Elizabeth said sarcastically. "I've never met dead men before."

"Watch your mouth, bitch!" Cy snapped.

"Calm down, Cy," Port said. "Don't let this sprout rankle you. Pa said she wasn't to be touched."

"Who's your Pa?" Elizabeth asked.

"You'll meet him soon enough," Port replied. He glanced at Burt. "Move out."

"Not yet," Elizabeth said.

Port stared at her. "What'd you say?"

"Not yet."

"Don't your ears work?" Port demanded. "Was I just wastin' my breath?"

"I've got to go," Elizabeth informed him.

"Go?" Port responded, clearly perplexed. "Go where?"

"You know," Elizabeth said modestly. "Go."

Port's brow creased. "Go where?" he reiterated.

"She's got to piss, lunkhead," the one called Boone said.

Port straightened. "I knew that," he said defensively.

"Cows fly too," Boone rejoined.

Port motioned with his right arm. "Get crackin', missy. We ain't got all day!"

Elizabeth's jaw muscles tensed. "You surely don't expect a lady to do her toilet in front of . . . of *men?*"

"We've all seen naked woman before," Port said. "It won't faze us none."

Elizabeth placed her hands on her hips. "I will not do it in front of brigands!"

"Brigands?" Port chuckled. "We're not Brigands. We're Bascombs."

Boone slapped his right thigh and shook his head, his curly hair bobbing. "She meant outlaws, stupid!"

Port, obviously uncomfortable, bristled. "You got no call to talk to me like that, Boone."

Boone grinned. "Don't take it personal, big brother. We both know you never had no book learnin'."

"And just 'cause you did don't make you no better than me," Port commented archly. He faced Elizabeth. "Now get to goin'."

"I will not."

"Then don't piss, for all I care," Port said.

Elizabeth turned her charms on the driver, the youngest one. "Isn't there at least one gentleman present? Is this any way to treat a lady, I ask you?"

Burt swiveled. "This ain't right."

Port wagged a thick finger at Burt. "Now don't you start, or I'll whup you proper!"

Burt's lean face reddened. "You try and see what happens!"

Boone moved his stallion closer to the wagon. "We don't have time for this, Port. Why not let her be about her business? Won't take but a minute."

Port surveyed the barren landscape. "Where's she goin' to go?"

"We could rig up somethin' with the blankets," Boone suggested.

Port nodded. He clambered from the wagon and removed two of the blankets from the flatbed. By draping the blankets over the right side of the wagon bed, then stretching them to the ground and securing them with rocks, he constructed a serviceable makeshift tent. "There! Now you git yourself under there and be done with it!"

"Not until you move away," Elizabeth said.

"What? You're loco, missy! Now hop to it!"

"No," Elizabeth balked.

Port clenched his huge fists. "I'm through playin' games with you, missy!" he threatened her.

"Be careful," Elizabeth reminded him. "Your pa said I wasn't to be touched!"

Port was furious.

"We can pull back a mite," Boone recommended. "She won't be goin' nowhere." He unlimbered a large rifle from a scabbard near his right leg. "I can hit a chipmunk at two hundred yards with this needle gun, girl. So don't get no funny notions in your head."

Burt jumped from the wagon, and the four men drifted to the rear about twenty yards.

"Get crackin'!" Port bellowed.

Elizabeth spotted a rag in a corner at the rear of the bed, grabbed it, then climbed to the ground. She crouched and moved under the blankets.

Twenty yards off, the one called Cy was stroking the stubble on his chin. "That bitch is trouble. I feel it in my bones."

"You fret too much," Boone said. "She's got spunk. I like that."

They waited.

And waited.

"What's takin' so long?" Port groused.

"Women need more time than men," Burt declared.

"Oh? How would you know?" Port demanded.

The blankets parted and Elizabeth appeared. She hoisted herself into the wagon.

"At last!" Port shuffled forward, joined by the others. Boone took his position on the right, Cy on the left, and Burt on the driver's seat.

Port unhooked the blankets and tossed them into the wagon. He glanced down at his feet, then at Elizabeth. "You gave us all that trouble for that little lump of shit? Hardly seems worth the bother."

# 5

An orderly appeared in the doorway to General Nels Demming's office at Fort Laramie. "Sir! There's a man here to see you."

"Not now," Demming responded. He was seated at his desk, absently gazing at the compound through his window, his mind overcome by his concern for his beloved daughter. The years of hardship in the military had taken their toll. Demming's broad face was lined with premature wrinkles, far more than an ordinary man of fifty-six would have. His hair was gray, balding at the top with thick sideburns tapered to a point. His brown eyes were pools of anxiety.

"Sir!" the orderly persisted. "Lieutenant James said it was important for you to see this man. It's about your daughter."

Demming straightened, turning his chair toward the door. "Then show him in, Private. Immediately."

The orderly disappeared.

Demming waited impatiently, drumming his fingers on his desk. He wondered if one of the scouts had found his daughter's abductors. Lieutenant James had ordered the Crow scouts to forge ahead of the rescue column, knowing the Indians could make better time on their speedy mustangs than the troopers could hope to achieve. One of the scouts, a brave called Lone Eagle, was responsible for determining Elizabeth's fate. After she had failed to appear at the dance hall, Demming had sent out men to scour the fort. Lone Eagle, the best of the trackers, had managed to read her sign, followed her prints into the field and detected the evidence of her kidnapping. Lone Eagle had maintained three men had jumped her in the high grass and carried her to a wagon. The fools! Demming fumed. How could they hope to escape his cavalry in a wagon?

Footsteps padded in the corridor.

Demming focused on the doorway.

A stranger slid into the room. He didn't walk. He didn't run. He seemed to glide into the office, to the right of the doorway, his back to the wall, his hands hooked in his gunbelt. The stranger was of average height and weight. He wore an unusual combination of clothing; a broad brimmed black *sombrero*, a Confederate butternut frock coat, black homespun pants, and knee-high Indian moccasins. His eyes, though, were his most striking feature. A peculiar shade of light blue with an eerie hypnotic quality. These eyes swept the room, and returned to the general.

"Who the hell are you?" Demming demanded. "And what the blazes do you know about my daughter?"

The stranger walked up to the general's wide desk. When he spoke, his voice was low, flinty. "If you want to see your daughter alive," his tone hardened, "don't ever talk to me like that again!"

Demming resisted an impulse to rise and punch the stranger in his smug face.

"The handle is Sherm," the stranger said.

"Sherm what?" Demming asked.

"Sherm is all you need to know," the man stated.

"You've got your gall," Demming remarked, "coming in here unarmed, addressing me like this!"

The stranger's right hand flashed in, then out, and Demming found himself gazing down the nickel plated barrel of an ivory handled 1851 Navy Colt. "Who said I was unarmed?"

Demming flinched. He'd seen many men draw their irons during his lengthy lifetime of serving on the fringe of civilization, but he could recall few as fast as this man calling himself Sherm.

The stranger grinned. Using his left hand, he lifted his

frock coat aside. Around his slim waist was a black sash. And there, its barrel angled under the silk sash, ivory grips poised for a quick draw, was the twin of the gun Sherm held in his right hand. He twirled the gun, then, in a practiced, fluid motion, eased it under the sash of his right side.

"Where's Beth?" Demming inquired.

Sherm studied the general. "She's safe. So far. But if you ever want to see her again, alive, you'd best do exactly what I say."

"What do you want?"

"We'll get to that." Sherm sat down on the edge of the general's oaken desk. "First thing, you call off your blue bellies."

"What?"

"You heard me," Sherm stated. "Call off your troops. We knew you'd catch up to us, us usin' a wagon and all. That's why I was waitin' for your men, miles from the wagon. Your scouts found me first, then Lieutenant James and his boys. James escorted me here, but your men are still waitin' out there, boilin' in the sun. I made it real clear. If they kept goin' my brothers would kill your girl. That plain enough for you?"

Demming's face was coated with sweat.

"Reckon so," Sherm said, smirking. "You should be grateful, General. At least we're allowin' your girl the comfort of a wagon. We could just as easily have tossed her over a horse and tied her arms and legs. But we didn't. We're right considerate, don't you think?"

Demming didn't reply.

"Anyhow," Sherm continued, "here's the way it lays. If we see anyone—*anyone*—doggin' our tail, your girl dies. Soldiers, Injuns, whatever, the girl dies. You try pickin' us off with sharpshooters, the girl dies. You try any tricks, the girl dies. If you don't let me leave, the girl dies. If you interfere with our plans in any way, the girl dies. You follow me?"

"What do you want?" Demming asked weakly. "I don't have much money, but what I have is yours. Just spare Beth."

Sherm grinned. "Your money? We didn't go to all this effort for nothin', Demming. We ain't interested in your money."

"Then what?"

Sherm stared at the officer. "We want the Wassleman gold."

General Demming did a double-take. "The what?"

"You need your ears cleaned?" Sherm rejoined. "The Wassleman gold. Don't bother playin' innocent with me. My Pa knows all about it. You know about it, too. Toward the end of the War, 1864 or thereabouts, a man in Denver by the name of Wassleman donated a million dollars to your damned Yankee cause! A million dollars in gold bars! You heard the story?"

General Demming nodded. "Everybody's heard it. But it's just a tall tale. There's no truth to it."

Sherm chuckled. "Sure. You keep lyin' to me, and your girl will come back to you in a pine box."

Demming's face became livid.

"We know what happened to the gold," Sherm continued. "You blue bellies decided to take it east. But you reckoned you'd be fancy about it, try to throw off us Rebs. So you went north, 'stead of due east, plannin' to swing east later. But the blue bellies escortin' the wagons was ambushed by Injuns in Ten Sleep Canyon. Only a few got out with their hides intact."

"Even if this absurd story were true," General Demming interrupted, "what does all this have to do with Beth?"

Sherm studied the general for a moment. "How did you ever get to be a General, with such a pitiful lack of brains?"

It took all of Demming's self control to restrain his raging temper.

"It's simple," Sherm said. "You deliver us the gold, and we hand over you precious daughter."

Demming could scarcely credit his hearing. "What?"

Sherm slowly stood. "That's the deal."

"You're insane!" Demming exclaimed. "There was no Wassleman gold! It's just a story, like so many others that sprang up during the War!"

Sherm yawned. "I warned you 'bout lyin' to me."

Demming didn't know what to say.

Sherm moved toward the doorway. He paused and glanced over his right shoulder. "We'll be in touch."

"Wait!" Demming cried. "You must listen to reason! Even if the gold existed, how would I know where it is?"

"My Pa knows the gold is buried in Ten Sleep Canyon. Check your records. You find the gold, General, or you'll never see your girl again."

General Demming stood. "How will I keep in touch with you?"

Sherm stopped. "You don't. We'll contact you when the time is ripe. Just be sure you have the gold."

"Don't harm my Beth," Demming declared.

Sherm grinned. "Or what?"

"Every man in the Wyoming Territory will be out looking for you. You'll never get away," Demming vowed.

"We ain't goin' nowhere 'till we get the gold," Sherm told him. "Remember to call off your blue bellies, and all the other law too. I also know 'bout the bounty you posted on us. Drop it, or I'll personally carve your daughter up and feed her to the coyotes." He stalked from the office.

"You bastards!" General Nels Demming was trembling from the intensity of his emotions. "You bastards! So help me God! If it's the last thing I ever do, I'll see every one of you scum dead!"

He sank into his chair, and for the first time since his wife had died sixteen years ago, tears formed in his eyes.

# 6

Preacher's powerful chestnut stallion ate up the miles. He headed north, sticking to the well traveled route between Cheyenne and Fort Laramie. He thought of the kidnapped daughter of General Demming, and of the sensational stories the Eastern newspapers would undoubtedly print about the abduction, and he was glad he wasn't involved. The damned newspapers had focused enough unwanted attention on his life. He idly wondered if any of the Eastern readers knew where Fort Laramie was located.

Most of them probably associated Laramie with the town of the same name located on the Laramie Plains fifty miles west of Cheyenne. The town had been founded by an American trapper named Jacques Laramie only the year before, in 1868, when the tracks of the Union Pacific reached it. But Fort Laramie was another matter, situated about seventy-five miles northeast of Cheyenne.

Preacher intended to ride north to the North Platte River, then swing to the northwest toward Ten Sleep. Considerable hard riding was involved, but the stallion was in his prime, and Preacher wanted to reach Ten Sleep as quickly as possible. He didn't anticipate encountering any delays.

He was wrong.

Preacher reached the Laramie River without incident, and forded its sluggish waters. He rode up a rise on the other side, and that was when he spotted the riders. Ten of them. Silhouetted against the blue sky, about a quarter of a mile distant.

Preacher wondered if they'd seen him.

The ten men suddenly broke into a gallop, coming in Preacher's direction.

Precher debated whether to fight or head for cover. He had his .58 caliber in his bedroll, but its range was inferior to a standard rifle. The .58, like his forty-four forties, had been crafted by a German gunsmith in Denver. Originally one of the last of the horse pistols manufactured by U.S. armories, the .58 was a throwback to the earlier cap and ball pistols. It used a detachable stock. Without the stock, it was seventeen inches long; with the stock, the .58 extended to over twenty-eight inches and served as a small carbine. The German gunsmith had converted the old .58 into a seven cartridge revolver with a blued barrel. The detachable stock was nickled. The recoil could break a man's wrist if he wasn't mighty cautious about how he used the gun.

The ten men were narrowing the gap.

Preacher recognized the unmistakable cut of military uniforms, and realized he was being approached by a cavalry patrol. He decided to wait and see what they wanted.

The patrol galloped up to the man in black and halted. A stern lieutenant was in charge. He nodded, scrutinizing the man in front of him. "Hello. I'm Lieutenant Standish. I need to know where you are heading."

"What business is it of yours?" Preacher replied.

Lieutenant Standish pursed his lips. He recognized trouble when he saw it. This man before him was obviously a gunman, and from the black attire, Standish judged him to be a gambler. Many of the professional gamblers were skilled shootists. They had to be, if they wanted to stay alive. "May I ask your name, sir?" Standish inquired politely.

"Preacher."

Standish stiffened. "Are you J.D. Preacher? The Widow Maker?"

Preacher nodded.

Standish twisted in his saddle and motioned to his men.

# SLAUGHTER AT TEN SLEEP 37

Immediately, they fanned out around the man in black, their carbines in their hands.

Preacher watched them with a detached air. There was no reason for the army to be interfering in his affairs, and he determined to get to the bottom of it.

"I'm sorry, Mister Preacher," Lieutenant Standish said, "but I'll have to ask for your guns."

"It's Preacher," the man in black corrected him. "There's no mister attached. And as for my guns—" He straightened, "You try taking them, and half of your men will be dead before I hit the ground."

Lieutenant Standish pondered a bit. "I suppose you can keep your guns. But I'm under orders to escort you to Fort Laramie, with or without your cooperation."

"Why Fort Laramie?" Preacher asked.

"I'm under orders from General Demming," Standish responded. "There are patrols out all over the place looking for you."

"General Demming? The one whose daughter was kidnapped?"

"The same, sir," Standish confirmed.

"What's he want with me?" Preacher questioned the officer.

Lieutenant Standish shrugged. "I don't rightly know, sir. You can take it up with General Demming when we reach Fort Laramie."

"Then let's make tracks," Preacher said.

The ride to Fort Laramie was uneventful. Standish seemed awed by Preacher's reputation and treated him respectfully.

Fort Laramie was a hub of activity. Patrols leaving. Patrols arriving. A cluster of buildings covered the land to the west of the fort; frame structures, a few log buildings, and a mixture of Indian tipis. The high walls of Fort Laramie loomed above the plain like a miniature mountain. Lieutenant Standish's patrol entered the open west gate, and the patrol reined in near the administrative complex.

"Through that door," Lieutenant Standish said, pointing, "you will find General Demming. Good luck. If we meet later, I'll buy you a drink."

"You're on," Preacher said, dismounting. He tied the stallion to the rail and ambled inside.

"May I help you, sir?" inquired a youthful orderly. He was sitting behind a small desk. Beyond him was a closed door.

"J.D. Preacher to see General Demming," Preacher stated.

The orderly gulped. "Yes, sir!" He rose and nearly tripped as he hurried to the door. After knocking once, he went inside. There was an exchange of voices, and the orderly emerged. "General Demming will see you now."

Preacher entered Demming's office. A man he took to be Demming was seated behind an oak desk. Two other men were in the room. One, a rugged lieutenant, was seated in a chair in front of the desk. The other, a colonel, was in a similar chair to Demming's left.

General Demming stood. "Is it true? Are you J.D. Preacher?"

"I am."

Demming's expression clouded. "What are you, man? An idiot? Or just a greedy son of a bitch?"

Preacher reached the desk in three strides. His right hand hovered near his hip gun. "You'd best have a good excuse for what you just said."

"A good excuse!" Demming exclaimed. "I have the best excuse in the world! My daughter is out there somewhere, in the hands of killers! And now you come along, threatening to force their hand! You'll excuse me if I don't pat you on the back!"

"What?" Preacher said, puzzled.

Demming leaned on his desk. "I know why you're here. Marshal Landry telegraphed us from Cheyenne. He told us you were coming after Elizabeth's abductors, that you're after the bounty. Well, I've got news for you, bounty hunter! The bounty has been rescinded until further notice!"

Preacher relaxed. "I'm not after the men who took your daughter."

Now it was General Demming's turn to appear bewildered. "You're not?"

"No. I heard about the kidnapping. The whole territory has. But I'm on personal business, headed for Ten Sleep," Preacher explained.

# SLAUGHTER AT TEN SLEEP

He liked the strength of character he saw in General Demming's features, and he could understand the general's reaction. He'd probably act the same way if he ever had a daughter. If. . . .

General Demming recovered quickly. "I'm sorry, Preacher," he apologized. "You've no idea the strain this is putting me through."

"I can imagine," Preacher said tactfully.

General Demming ran his right hand through his tousled hair. "I haven't slept a wink. I don't know what to do." He glanced at Preacher. "I need professional advice, and you're just the man to give it."

"Me?"

"You're a bounty hunter, aren't you? You've killed, what did I hear? Two dozen men? What do you say? Will you hear me out?"

Preacher was about to decline, but his mind filled with haunting images of Abby. Dear, sweet Abby. His sister. Raped and tortured by the carpetbaggers responsible for killing his father and mother. Abigail survived, only to be sadistically brutalized and murdered in Empire, Colorado, by one of the men riding with his brother, Zack.

"I'll give a listen," he replied.

General Demming brightened. "Excellent. I'd like you to meet two of my officers. This is Colonel McCarty."

Preacher nodded at the heavy set colonel with the jowly chin.

"And this is Lieutenant James. He's just in from the field. He was the one who caught up with one of Beth's kidnappers," Demming said.

"You caught one of them?" Preacher asked.

"Not exactly," General Demming stated. "One moment." He glanced at the doorway to his office. "Orderly!" he bellowed.

The orderly zipped into view. "Yes, sir!"

"A chair for Preacher here! On the double!" Demming ordered.

"Yes, sir!"

It took all of thirty seconds for the orderly to return with a chair, then leave.

"Now then," General Demming said as Preacher took his

seat. "I'd best start at the beginning. I know the wires have spread the news all over the Territory and to points east. Those damn reporters are hovering around the fort like vultures over a buffalo carcass. Half the stuff they print isn't even accurate."

"I'm not too fond of reporters myself," Preacher interjected.

"Then you know what I mean," Demming said. "Now about Beth. The last time I saw her was last night, at the house I've rented for us outside the fort. It's not much, but it's better than the spartan accommodations the Army normally provides. I thought I'd give her a treat."

He paused. "Last night I was hosting a formal dance. Beth loves to dance, Preacher. Takes after her mother, God rest her soul. I left early to attend to the dance. Beth wanted to be alone, to get all gussied up for the affair. She said she'd join me at the hall in an hour. She never arrived."

Demming frowned, the strain showing. "I sent Lieutenant James to the house, but Beth wasn't there. Naturally, I had my men search the fort. One of my scouts, Lone Eagle, was able to track Beth from our front door into a field about forty yards away. We used a dozen lanterns to light the ground. Thank God we had a light rain early last evening. The dirt was easy to read."

"What did this scout find?" Preacher queried.

"Indications of a struggle. Three men evidently ambushed my poor Beth and loaded her into a wagon. There was another man waiting in the street, holding their getaway mounts. Add a wagon driver, and we're likely dealing with four or five men, tops. They headed west. I ordered my men out. The trail was easy to follow." He looked at the rugged Lieutenant. "You should take over the telling.

"Yes, sir. But there's not much to tell. Our scouts took the lead. They were about fifteen miles from the fort when they found one of the kidnappers waitin' for 'em," Lieutenant James detailed.

"Waiting?" Preacher reiterated.

"Yep. Just sittin' there on his horse, smack dab in the middle of the wagon tracks. He waited there for the column. Then he warned us not to proceed. Said if we went any further, Miss Demming would die. I had my men wait, and brought the man to see the general," James concluded.

"The most upstart son of a bitch you'd ever want to meet!" General Demming exploded. "Waltzed into *my* office and dictated their terms to me! Told me Beth would die if we tried any tricks."

"This son of a bitch have a name?" Preacher asked.

Demming nodded. "Called himself Sherm. No last name. Said his brothers were with Beth. Said they'd kill her if we attempted anything. ANYTHING. That's why I had patrols scouring the countryside for you. I was frantic after Marshal Landry wired us, saying you were coming after the bounty on Beth's kidnappers. I knew they'd kill her if they knew you were after them. No hard feelings?"

Preacher shook his head. "None. I'd of done the same, if I was in your boots. Tell me more about this Sherm. What was he like?"

General Demming snorted. "Fancied himself a gunman. Wears a pair of Colts in a waist sash, just like Wild Bill Hickok. He's fast, though. I won't deny that."

"He pulled on you?" Preacher asked in surprise.

Demming nodded. "He had to show off. Show me what he could do. He'd outdraw most men I know."

"Why'd they take your daughter, General?" Preacher inquired.

General Demming wearily shook his head, frowning. "That's the crazy part! They want to exchange her for a million in gold bars."

"A million in gold bars? I think you're right. They must be loco," Preacher said.

"You haven't heard the half of it!" Demming exclaimed. "They want the Wassleman gold!"

"The Wassleman gold?" Preacher repeated.

"That's right. You didn't serve in these parts during the War, did you?" Demming asked.

"I spent most of it with Mosby's Rangers," Preacher disclosed. "We stuck pretty much to the East."

"Then you haven't heard about the Wassleman gold?"

Preacher shook his head.

"I heard the story, of course," General Demming said, "but I can't vouch for its authenticity. The bare bones facts are these. Back in '64, a man in Denver by the name of Ezra Wassleman decided to donate a million dollars to the Union Treasury. Wassleman reportedly made his money from a mine in the Colorado Rockies. Found a rich lode, he did, and accumulated about twelve million before the lode petered out. The Army was to transport the million, in the form of gold bars, back east. The wagon train carrying the money traveled north out of Denver, intending to bear eastward when they were well beyond the range of Confederate patrols. In or near Ten Sleep Canyon, they were attacked by a Cheyenne war party. Only a few of the troopers managed to escape with their lives after burying the gold." Demming paused. "The newspapers never reported it, but perhaps the army wanted it hushed up. That's the story, anyway."

"Think there's any truth to it?" Preacher asked.

"I don't know," General Demming replied. "I doubt it. You know how these wild tales are started. Lost mines. Lost payrolls. Buried treasure. Spanish gold. There must be dozens of such stories. I heard the Wassleman tale at a dinner party from a fellow officer half under the table. What man in his right mind credits such drivel?"

"The kidnappers must," Preacher said, "if they went to all the trouble of taking your daughter."

Demming scowled. "There's the rub! I have my staff checking on the story. If, as I expect, it turns out to be phony, how can I convince the kidnappers of that? How can I stop them from harming Beth? They'd never believe a word I say."

"You've got a stickler," Preacher agreed.

General Demming leaned forward, his elbows on his desk. "I might have a chance to save Beth with your help."

"I thought you didn't want me sticking my nose in," Preacher reminded him.

"I didn't," Demming admitted, "but I've been thinking it over while we talked. Perhaps I was hasty. One man, a skilled bounty hunter, say, might be able to do what an entire regiment couldn't. What do you say?"

"Sounds risky to me," Preacher said.

"There are risks no matter what course I take," General Demming stated. "If I do nothing, they might kill Beth. She might be able to identify them, and they wouldn't want that. If I send my men after her, they'll kill her for sure. Even if, by some miracle, the Wassleman story turned out to be true and I found the gold for them, they might kill her anyway."

He suddenly pounded the desk with his right fist. "Damn it! I can't be expected to do nothing! That's my little girl out there! All I have left!"

Preacher noticed the acute worry reflected in Lieutenant James' face. He wondered if the lieutenant was concerned about the general, or the general's daughter?

"What do you say, Preacher?" General Demming asked. "Will you help me?"

Preacher hesitated.

"I'll pay you!" Demming offered. "You know about the five thousand I posted. The kidnappers made me call it off. But I'll hand it over to you, every penny of it, if you'll only bring my Beth back alive! Will you?"

"I can try," Preacher responded, "but I can't make any promises. It'll be ticklish."

The orderly appeared in the doorway. "General Demming?"

Demming looked up. "What is it? I'm busy. I don't want to be disturbed unless there's word of my daughter."

"But you said this was important, sir." The orderly was holding a sheet of paper in his right hand.

"What have you got there?" Demming demanded.

The orderly waved the paper. "It's a dispatch, sir. The one you've been waiting for on the Wassleman gold."

General Demming rose and hurried to the orderly. He took the report, dismissed the orderly, and began reading it as he returned to his desk. He was halfway across the room when he stopped near Preacher's chair and grimaced. "Dear God! It's true!"

"There really was a shipment of gold?" Preacher asked.

Demming nodded. "It says here the bars were in three wagons. The Indians surrounded the wagon train, and the troopers dug in. For four days the fight went on, with the Cheyenne picking off the soldiers one by one. The officer in charge, a Major Mason, had his men bury the bars at night, when the Indians couldn't see into the gully the men occupied. On the fifth day, the Cheyenne made a concerted rush on the troopers left. Only two escaped. One of them was wounded and later died. The other man was taken back with two hundred cavalry, but they couldn't find the gold."

"They couldn't find it?" Colonel McCarty finally spoke

up.

General Demming lowered the dispatch. "Ten Sleep Canyon is big. Lots of hiding places. Ravines, gorges, gullies. To top it off, the wagon train was traveling at night. The last trooper had no idea where they were when they were hit. The army searched and searched. Nothing."

"Wasn't there any sign of the wagons and the bodies?" Lieutenant James asked.

"No," General Demming answered. "Their fate is a mystery. The Indians may have taken the wagons or burned them to the ground. They probably stripped the troopers, took all their clothes and weapons. The scavengers would have disposed of the corpses rather quickly."

"What about the last soldier?" Preacher inquired. "Is he still around?"

General Demming frowned. "No. He was killed in action. He'd been assigned to Fort Phil Kearny, and was one of those wiped out along with Captain Fetterman by Red Cloud and his bunch."

"What are your plans, sir?" Lieutenant James questioned him.

General Demming thought for a moment. He stared at Preacher. "I have to put my trust in you. There's no other choice. If I can buy you some time, do you think you can save my daughter from these madmen?"

"I reckon," Preacher replied, "but how do you aim to buy me some time?"

"The kidnappers expect me to retrieve the gold from Ten Sleep Canyon. I won't disappoint them. I'll take a column up there and search for the gold. It's unlikely we'll find anything, but I'd be willing to bet they'll have someone watching us. If I drag out the operation, it should give you the time you need to find them."

General Demming's eyes lit up. "You know, maybe I misjudged Beth's captors. They might not be so dumb after all."

"How do you figure?" Preacher asked.

"Look at it from their angle," General Demming said. "If there's only four or five of them, they could spend a lifetime searching Ten Sleep Canyon and never come close to locating the gold. But a hundred soldiers might succeed, especially with the right incentive."

"And what better incentive," Lieutenant James concluded grimly, "than knowin' the life of their commander's daughter hung in the balance?"

"Like I said," General Demming remarked. "I may have misjudged them. They're not completely insane." He bent over, his face close to Preacher's. "There's something I want you to do for me, bounty hunter. No matter what happens out there, you do it."

"Do what?" Preacher inquired, knowing the answer before he posed the question.

General Demming's features hardened, became granite. "Kill them, Preacher. Kill every fucking one of them!"

# 7

"How much farther do we have to go?" Elizabeth demanded.

They were stopped for the night in a shallow ravine to hide them from hostile eyes and shelter them from the whipping wind.

"Don't fret none, missy," Port chided her. "We'll get there when we get there."

"And where is *there*?" Elizabeth asked.

"Nosy bitch, ain't she?" Cy commented from the other side of the fire.

Port, Cy and Burt were lounging around the campfire. Boone was off keeping watch.

Elizabeth glared at Cy Bascomb. "I'll thank you to address me civilly!"

Cy snickered. "Or what, bitch?"

Elizabeth turned her lovely eyes on the youngest Bascomb. "Why do you allow him to belittle me so?"

Burt, her ever ready knight in shining armor, glanced at Cy. "You leave off her, Cy. You hear me?"

Cy glanced at Port. "Do you believe this shithead? The bitch farts, and he thinks it's perfume!"

Port laughed uproariously.

Burt leaped to his feet. "I'm warnin' you!"

Cy placed his plate of beans on the ground and slowly

stood. "Don't be bitin' off more than you can chew, little brother."

Burt Bascomb's right hand was perched near the .44 caliber Colt Dragoon on his right hip.

Cy Bascomb was armed with a Model 1860 Army Colt revolver, also a .44 caliber, in a Mexican loop holster, butt extended for a cross draw, on his left hip.

"Now you boys hold on!" Port declared, rising.

"Butt out!" Cy snapped. "This don't concern you."

A new voice, a low, menacing voice, interjected, "Does it concern me?"

Everyone turned.

Elizabeth was startled to find Boone Bascomb and one other man standing on the sloping ravine behind her. The newcomer wore a black *sombrero*, a Confederate frock coat, and black pants and moccasins. The firelight glinted off the ivory grips of a pair of Colts secured by a waist sash.

"Sherm!" Cy exclaimed nervously. "We didn't hear you come up."

The one called Sherm descended into camp, his body moving with a pantherish gait. "Who you joshin'? You assholes were makin' so much noise, a herd of buffalo could have stampeded right over you without you knowin' it!"

Boone laughed.

Sherm Bascomb walked right up to Cy. "Did my eyes deceive me? Or were you 'bout to pull on brother Burt?"

Cy tried to laugh, but it came off as a strangled titter. "I would never do that. You know I wouldn't."

Sherm took three steps backwards, his thumbs hooked in his black sash. "Do I? Tell you what I'll do. If you're so all fired keen to draw on somebody I'll let you pull on me."

"What?" Cy asked in a whisper.

"Now hold on, Sherm," Port objected.

"You keep your mouth shut, Port, or I'll give you the same chance," Sherm stated.

Port shook his head. "I'll pass."

Elizabeth was mesmerized by this Sherm Bascomb. He seemed to be endowed with a magnetic air. The man in the *sombrero* radiated danger from every pore. She instinctively sensed the other Bascombs, with the exception of Boone, feared Sherm.

"Whenever you're ready, Cy," Sherm said.

Cy raised his arms to chest height. "I won't pull on you, Sherm. You're kin!"

"Isn't Burt kin, too?" Sherm demanded.

"Sure he is," Cy responded.

"Then I don't want to ever see you 'bout to draw on him, Cy," Sherm said, "or I'll kill you my own self. Any objections?"

Cy shook his head. "I'd never hurt Burt! Honest! But the bitch there has got him jumpin' every time she whines!"

"Is that a fact?" Sherm Bascomb turned and gazed upon their captive for the first time. He'd seen her only briefly during the kidnapping, and he'd rode off to intercept their pursuit before she was freed from the blankets. He admired her long raven hair and the shapely contours of her dress. "Howdy, ma'am. I'm called Sherm."

"I gathered," Elizabeth replied. She tried to read his age, and estimated he wasn't much older than she, not by more than four or five years.

"You been givin' us trouble?" Sherm inquired politely.

"What do you expect after the manner in which I've been treated?" Elizabeth responded indignantly.

Sherm walked up to her, grinning. "My brothers been givin' you a hard time?"

"They haven't molested me, if that's what you mean," Elizabeth said.

"Nobody is goin' to molest you," Sherm said. "We ain't interested in your body, Miss Demming."

"Why did you abduct me?" Elizabeth asked.

"For gold, Miss Demming. More gold than anybody's ever seen at one time in one place. Your papa's goin' to help us get it," Sherm informed her.

"How?" Elizabeth inquired.

"Forget her!" Port interrupted. "How'd it go at Fort Laramie?"

"Yeah. How did it go?" Boone added.

Sherm gazed at his brothers, smiling. "I laid the law down for General Demming . . ."

"You saw my father?" Elizabeth exclaimed.

"Sure did," Sherm admitted. "He said I should pass on his love."

"Really?" Elizabeth beamed. "What else?"

"He said for you to behave yourself," Sherm stated, "and

## SLAUGHTER AT TEN SLEEP

he'll get you out of this safe and sound."

"Will the blue bellies be givin' us any grief?" Cy inquired.

"Doubt it," Sherm replied. "Demming knows what'd happen."

"How long do you reckon we'll have to wait?" Port queried.

"That's up to the blue bellies." Sherm grinned at Elizabeth. "But I don't figure them to be draggin' their heels."

"Pa will be pleased," Port said.

Sherm glanced around the camp. "I wouldn't gamble on it."

"Why not?" Port asked.

"Where do you keep your brains, Port? In that big gut of yours? What's Pa goin' to say when we show up without Rafe and Rufus?" Sherm responded.

"We never should of let them ride to Cheyenne," Burt said.

"They wanted to go," Sherm said. "They hadn't been there in 'bout nine months. I didn't think it would do no harm."

"They should of been back ages ago," Port commented, gazing to the southeast.

"What do you figure happened to 'em?" Burt asked.

"No way of tellin'," Sherm answered. "They're most likely up to their armpits in women and drink. We'll fetch 'em later. Right now, the important thing is to take Miss Demming to Pa."

"Where are you taking me?" Elizabeth asked.

Sherm pointed to the northwest. "Ten Sleep. Ever been there?"

Elizabeth shook her head.

"It's a nice little town," Sherm said. "It's *our* town, Miss Demming. Lock, stock, and barrel. So don't be gettin' any notions 'bout someone there helpin' you. When we get there, you keep quiet, you hear?"

"I will," Elizabeth promised, lying. She intended to scream for help the first chance she got.

"You'd better," Sherm stated. "Just remember. In case you get any funny notions, I'll kill anyone who interferes with our plans. That plain enough for you?"

"Couldn't be plainer," Elizabeth conceded.

"Good." Sherm squatted next to the fire. "Ummm. Those beans sure smell good! Did you do the cookin', Port?"

"Who else?" Port replied.

"Have you tasted any of this, Miss Demming?" Sherm asked.

"I wasn't hungry," Elizabeth said stiffly.

"You'd be doin' yourself a favor if you tried 'em," Sherm said. "Ol' Port is a wizard with the grub."

Port grinned appreciately. "No more than you are with the Colts, Sherm."

Sherm lifted the lid on the pot. "Smell that! It makes my mouth water!"

He stared up at Elizabeth Demming, and her prominent breasts. The grub wasn't the only thing making his mouth water.

# 8

Preacher stayed off the beaten track after he departed Fort Laramie. He rode north, fording the North Platte River, then swung northwesterly. His plan was to push as hard as he dared to outdistance the kidnappers and reach a vantage point in front of them. Elizabeth Demming's abductors would be concentrating on their back trail. They might not pay as much attention to the land in front of them.

The stallion plowed tirelessly onward. The rolling motion of his mount, combined with the incredible beauty of the landscape, combined to soothe Preacher's troubled soul. He thought less and less of Zack and poor Abby. The sweeping vistas, the stark red ridges, the budding flowers and the sage, washed over his senses, cleansing his mind of regrets and recriminations. He passed a herd of several hundred buffalo grazing near a stream, some of the belligerent bulls standing six feet at the shoulder and weighing up to two thousand pounds. Red tailed hawks and golden eagles soared on the air currents overhead. Pronghorns would dart aside at his approach, making fantastic bounds as they sped away, vaulting twenty feet at a leap. Ground Squirrels and Prairie Dogs yipped at him.

Preacher found it easy to comprehend why men like Hickok and Cody loved the plains. Wyoming Territory wasn't as green, as lush, as his native Tennessee. But despite its lack of prolific vegetation, the land held an undeniable charm, gripping a man deep in his being and never letting go. It wasn't for nothing that Hickok and company were referred to in the pulps as *Plainsmen.* Occasionally, the hack writers accidentally got something right.

Preacher spent the first night in a dry creek bed. He was up at the crack of dawn. After a few sips from his canteen and two pieces of jerky, he mounted up and resumed his journey.

Noon came and went. Preacher rode on.

Tall grass swayed in the field ahead. He was bearing to the northwest as he traveled, always to the northwest. He passed well north of the settlement of Douglas and, some miles further, Fort Fetterman. General Demming had been emphatic about the secrecy of Preacher's mission, and Preacher tended to agree. The kidnappers might have spies stationed at any of the settlements. All it would take was for one person to recognize Preacher as the infamous bounty hunger, and Elizabeth Demming's life wouldn't be worth a plugged nickel.

Preacher found a suitable arroyo for his second night's camp site and turned in. In the distance, a coyote was yapping at the moon.

Another hasty breakfast, another early departure, and the man in black resumed his trek. Two hours later he capped a hill and reined in, affording his horse a much deserved rest. He surveyed the grass and shrub below the hill, alert for Indian signs.

A raucous shouting erupted to his rear.

Preacher twisted in his saddle, astonished to discover at least twenty Cheyenne warriors surging up the hill. The foremost warrior wasn't more than fifty yards distant. They must have been dogging his trail, biding their time, slowly and silently narrowing the gap.

Now it was a race to the death.

Preacher spurred the stallion on, racing down the hill and across the fields beyond. For the next seven miles it was nip and tuck as the Cheyenne braves hounded him, their mustangs speeding through the tall grass on his heels. Preacher gradually pulled ahead, his powerful stallion effortlessly forging forward and increasing the distance between Preacher and his pursuers.

# SLAUGHTER AT TEN SLEEP

A creek appeared ahead, and forest loomed on the west bank. Preacher splashed across the water and up a steep bank, dodging the tree trunks as he rode deep into the woods. The trees would also serve to impede the Indians.

After an hour, he emerged from the forest into a rocky gorge. A deer trail wound into the gorge, and Preacher elected to take it. He skirted a huge boulder on his right and entered a small clearing. Something scraped to Preacher's right.

Preacher turned, the motion saving his life as a knife swept past his face and a burly body crashed into his, knocking him from his horse. He hurtled to the ground, his assailant on top, and it wasn't until he landed on his back, his attacker's right knee planted in his stomach, that Preacher recognized the man on top of him as a Cheyenne warrior.

The brave stabbed his knife at Preacher's neck. Preacher jerked his head aside, the knife thudding into the earth not an inch from his skin. He balled his right hand and struck the warrior on the chin. The brave toppled to the left.

Preacher rolled and came up with his hip gun in his right hand, but the Indian was ready for him.

The brave kicked with his left leg, his foot slamming into the white man's right wrist and jarring the forty-four forty loose. Instantly, the warrior pressed his advantage, slashing with his knife, striving to disembowel his enemy.

Preacher backed off, his arms flung wide to avoid the sweeping blade, unable to pull his vest gun or his Bowie. His left foot caught on a rock and he sprawled onto his back.

The Cheyenne brave whooped and leaped.

Preacher, flat on his back, drew his right leg in to his chest and kicked, striking the brave in the chest and sending him flying. The Barnes .50 boot pistol was jostled by the impact. It wriggled into view, and Preacher snatched it as the warrior jumped to his feet.

The brave pounced.

Preacher fired, the pistol roaring, the recoil jolting his right arm.

The Cheyenne warrior was hit in the chest, the impact bowling him over. He wound up on his back, on top of a flat rock, his blood spurting from the cavity in his chest.

Preacher stood. How the blazes had the Cheyenne caught

up with him? He realized the braves must know the country like the palms of their hands. They might have sent a few braves ahead, bypassing the forest, while the majority chased Preacher into the trees. If that was true, he reasoned, then there might be more braves lurking about.

There were.

A footfall sounded behind him.

Preacher whirled, dropping the empty .50 caliber hideout and pulling his vest gun.

Another Cheyenne warrior was charging the bounty hunter, waving some sort of war club.

Preacher shot the brave dead with one shot between the eyes. And then a funny thing happened. Something or someone smashed into Preacher's back, and he hurtled forward, going down on his hands and knees, dazed. He shook his head, trying to clear it, and saw a shadowy form appear to his right.

It was another Cheyenne armed with a tomahawk.

Preacher instinctively ducked to his left. He felt the tomahawk blade bite into his left shoulder, and he twisted and weaved, attempting to roll out of range. He came up onto his knees, and one of the flat sides of the tomahawk smacked him on the forehead, drawing blood, propelling him onto his back. He blinked, trying to clear his vision.

The Cheyenne brave straddled the white man's body and raised his tomahawk for the death stroke.

Preacher, dizzy, blood flowing over his eyes, swore he saw a spear or lance streak out of nowhere and impale the Cheyenne, penetrating the warrior's torso and extending a foot beyond. He struggled to prop himself on his elbows, and that was when the lights went out.

# 9

"Did you hear somethin'?" Port asked the others.

"Like what?" Sherm responded.

"A shot. Off that-a-way," Port said, pointing to the northeast.

"You're hearin' things," Burt remarked.

The wagon was following a dusty road—if you could call the dirt track a road—to the northwest. Burt handled the team. Port, as usual, rode with Elizabeth in the wagon bed. Boone, on his black stallion, was fifty yards to the east. Cy, on his brown mare, kept pace an equal distance to the west. Sherm Bascomb, on a frisky black mare with a white star on its forehead, rode alongside the wagon.

"Would you care for some water?" Sherm asked Elizabeth.

"No, thank you," Elizabeth declined. Sherm had allowed her to drink from his canteen only an hour before. He was paying particular attention to her every need, and she didn't know whether to be flattered or frightened. She did know the youngest, Burt, was seething with jealousy, and she schemed how she might turn the situation to her advantage.

"I hope we don't run into any Cheyenne," Port commented.

"You scared of Injuns, are you?" Sherm quipped.

"Anyone in their right mind is scared of Injuns," Port

replied.

"What would happen if we were attacked by Cheyenne?" Elizabeth asked. "There aren't enough of you to protect me."

"Don't you fret your pretty head about it, Miss Demming," Sherm told her. "I'd just swing you up behind me. Ol' Belle here can outrun any other horse there is."

"I hope so," Elizabeth said.

The heat intensified as the day progressed. Sherm called a temporary halt in the middle of the afternoon to rest the horses. The Bascomb brothers gathered around the wagon.

"Shouldn't we send somebody back?" Cy asked. "Them blue bellies might try to sneak up on us."

"If you're worried," Sherm responded, "you go back. Me, I can't see the lousy Yankees doin' anything to endanger Miss Demming."

"I'll be happy when we reach Ten Sleep," Burt mentioned wistfully.

"At this pace," Boone said, "it'll take another eight or ten days to reach it."

"We are movin' mighty slow," Sherm commented thoughtfully.

"It's this damn wagon," Cy complained. "If we ditched it, we could ride to Ten Sleep in half the time."

"Now there's a notion I like," Sherm concurred.

"Won't Pa be upset if we leave the wagon?" Burt inquired.

"Why should he be?" Sherm replied. "It's not like it's ours. We stole it in Fort Laramie, remember?"

"All Pa said was to bring the bitch back unharmed," Cy observed. "The wagon was Sherm's idea."

"It worked, didn't it?" Sherm said. "The blue bellies figured we'd be easy pickings in a wagon. They didn't come on as fast as they might have, thinkin' they'd catch up to us real quick like. It bought us a little extra time, and that's what counts."

"Then let's leave the wagon and hightail it to Ten Sleep," Boone proposed.

Sherm stared at Elizabeth. "I like the idea. You can ride with me, Miss Demming."

Elizabeth thought fast. "If you don't mind, I'd be more comfortable riding one of those." She pointed at one of the four horses comprising the wagon team.

"Suit yourself," Sherm said, sounding peeved.

The Bascombs hurriedly unhitched the team. Elizabeth mounted a brown mare. Boone volunteered to lead the other three horses.

"Head out!" Sherm directed.

The Bascombs started off at a brisk pace. Sherm fell in beside their prisoner. "You ride bareback real well, Miss Demming," he complimented her.

"Lots of practice," Elizabeth replied. "I've been riding since I was eight."

"You much of a cook?" Sherm idly asked.

"Probably not as good as Port," Elizabeth responded.

Sherm grinned. "And a sense of humor, too. Yep. You have a lot of admirable qualities. A man could do worse."

Elizabeth repressed a shiver. Sherm Bascomb was obviously intent on wooing her. Her intuition had been right. She found him oddly attractive, but she feared him too. The idea of finding herself alone with him frightened her. She perceived he wasn't one to respect womanhood, not where it really mattered.

"Maybe we shouldn't be sendin' you back to your father," Sherm said in a joking tone. "Maybe I should ask Pa if we can keep you for ourselves."

Elizabeth's grip on the reins tightened. Boone Bascomb had fashioned a makeshift bridle from the team harness.

"What do you think of the notion?" Sherm inquired.

"It isn't what I think that counts," Elizabeth answered.

"It isn't?" Sherm said, surprised.

"It's what my papa things that matters," Elizabeth told him. "And *he* wouldn't like the idea."

"He'd never know," Sherm stated.

"He'd find out," Elizabeth declared. "He'll find me sooner or later. I bet he has the entire U.S. Army out looking for me right this instant," she boasted.

"You do, huh?" Sherm said, grinning.

"I do," Elizabeth affirmed.

"There's no arguin' with a lady," Sherm said laughing.

# 10

Preacher slowly came awake, his consciousness swirling. He couldn't seem to focus properly. Try as he might, he couldn't recall what had happened. He vaguely recollected something about the army and a missing woman. Disjointed images flitted through his mind. A name popped up. Demming. General Nels Demming. And then another name. Elizabeth Demming. Suddenly, everything was remembered with startling clarity; the ride from Fort Laramie, the Cheyenne war party, and the fight in the gorge. His eyes snapped open and he sat up.

"Lie down, please!" said a soft feminine voice.

Preacher scanned his surroundings. He was in a tipi, covered with a buffalo robe. His shirt, hat, frock coat, and forty-four forties were lying in a pile near his right arm. The tipi flaps had been tied up, allowing sunshine to flood the interior. And he wasn't alone.

An Indian woman was kneeling to his left. "How you feel?" she inquired in melodious, accented English.

"I've felt better," Preacher acknowledged. His head was throbbing. He reached up and probed his forehead with his fingers. There was a tender knot in the center of his forehead. Above the bump was an indentation where his scalp had been split by the tomahawk blow. Preacher realized he'd been lucky. If the Cheyenne brave had caught him with the bladed edge of the tomahawk instead of the flat edge, Preacher's career would have been abruptly terminated. Preacher went to shift his position and a severe twinge racked his left shoulder. He gingerly examined the wound, a two-inch gash, and studied the herbal compress someone had applied.

"You do this?" he asked.

The Indian woman nodded. "You very hurt. Much fever. Take much medicine."

Preacher wondered if he'd developed an infection from one of the two wounds. "I want to thank you kindly for tending me. How long have I been here?"

"Four days," the woman replied.

She was young, in her early twenties perhaps, with luxuriant black hair flowing to the middle of her buckskin clad back. Her large dark eyes watched his every move. She had a pointed chin and rosy lips.

"Where am I?" Preacher inquired. He doubted he was in a Cheyenne camp. The warriors would have finished him off.

"Buffalo camp of Nez Perce," she answered.

Which explained a lot. The Nez Perce were not Plains Indians like the Cheyenne or Sioux. They dwelt far to the northwest, beyond the Yellowstone, but they frequently crossed to the plains to hunt buffalo. Sometimes bands of Nez Perce would remain on the plains for two years at a stretch. The Nez Perce were not warlike. Many of the experienced white scouts considered the Nez Perce to be among the very friendliest of tribes.

"What is your name?" Preacher asked her.

"Wallowa. Yours?"

"Preacher," he replied.

"Only Preacher? White men have big names. Yours same?" Wallowa said.

Preacher almost grinned. "I reckon you got me there. My folks named me Jeremy James David Preacher."

Wallowa smiled. "See?"

"How did I get here?" Preacher inquired.

"Red Echo bring," Wallowa said.

"Who's Red Echo? Kin of yours?"

"Red Echo father," Wallowa revealed.

"Where am I?" Preacher needed to know. "Where's this

camp?"

"Nez Perce camp on Crazy Woman Creek," Wallowa responded.

A shadow filled the tipi entrance, and a tall Nez Perce entered. He wore buckskins. His braided hair fell past his broad shoulders. His oval face conveyed an impression of honesty, of noble character. He exchanged words in the Nez Perce tongue with Wallowa.

"Red Echo glad you better," Wallowa translated.

"Tell Red Echo I'm in his debt," Preacher said. "I figure I owe him for my life."

Wallowa relayed the message and Red Echo responded.

"Red Echo says Spirit smiled on you," Wallowa stated.

"There's something I'd like to know," Preacher said.

"Yes?"

"Ask Red Echo why he saved me? Why save a white man in a fight with another Indian?" Preacher asked.

Wallowa averted her gaze. "Can answer for him. Nez Perce and Cheyenne are—" she made a motion with her hands, as if she was breaking a stick, "with much bad blood. Also," her voice lowered, "Cheyenne kill Wallowa's husband. A white man."

"You were married to a white man?"

"Yes. Trapper man. George Wheeler," she said proudly, and somewhat sadly.

"Sorry to hear it," Preacher remarked. He looked up at Red Echo. "How can I repay him for saving my life?"

Wallowa and Red Echo talked a bit. Finally, Wallowa turned to Preacher. "You must decide."

"We can start by being friends," Preacher proposed, extending his right hand.

Red Echo stared at Preacher's hand for a moment, then shook it awkwardly, smiling as he did. He nodded and left the tipi.

"You hungry?" Wallowa said. "Have venison stew."

"Bring it on," Preacher said.

Wallowa departed.

Preacher rummaged through his piled clothing. He found his precious Bowie under his hat and the Barnes .50 caliber inside his folded frock coat. The sight of the Barnes gave him an idea.

Wallowa returned with a heaping clay bowl of steaming

SLAUGHTER AT TEN SLEEP 61

venison stew. She stayed on her knees, her eyes constantly on his face, as Preacher wolfed the food. The stew was delicious, and he showed his appreciation by smacking his lips when he finished.

"You like?" Wallowa asked.

"Never had better," Preacher told her.

Wallowa seemed inordinately pleased by his comment. She took the bowl and exited, humming to herself.

Preacher eased onto his back. The food felt good, giving his stomach a tight, well-fed sensation. He pondered his next move.

Going after Elizabeth Demming's kidnappers in his current state was out of the question. He needed to be in top form if he was going to face four or five killers. And there really wasn't any urgency to his mission, at least for the time being. The kidnappers wouldn't be stupid enough to harm the girl before they received the gold. No girl, no gold. So Elizabeth was safe until her abductors ran out of patience, waiting for General Demming to find the stash.

Preacher rubbed his sore left shoulder. He knew the kidnappers had been bearing to the northwest, and he speculated on their ultimate destination. There were any number of settlements they could hole up in. They could even pitch camp on the prairie in some secluded spot, keeping Elizabeth away from civilization and possible discovery. So how was he to find them in the vast expanse of the Wyoming Territory? His original plan, to ride ahead of them and spy on them from a high mesa or ridge, was no longer feasible. Cutting their sign would have been easy within two or three days of Fort Laramie. Now, it would be almost impossible.

So how was he to find them?

Preacher recalled something General Demming had said, shortly before Preacher rode from the fort. *I don't know when I'll hear from Beth's kidnappers. That bastard, Sherm, told me they'd be in touch when the time was ripe.*

What did that mean? When the time was ripe? When General Demming had located the stashed gold bars? But how would the kidnappers know the gold was found, unless they figured to post one of their men in the vicinity of Demming's soldiers and spy on the search? That made sense. The kidnappers would want to know, pronto, if

Demming located the gold.

Preacher nodded. He knew what his next step would be.

Wallowa entered the tipi bearing a water jug. "Here. Drink deep," she advised.

Preacher rose on his right elbow. "I can't thank you enough." He took the jug and swallowed the clear, cool liquid.

"There may be way," Wallowa said, grinning sheepishly.

Three more days Preacher stayed with the Nez Perce. Under Wallowa's skillful ministrations, his wounds healed rapidly. The herbs she applied relieved the pain and reduced the swelling. She waited on him hand and foot. She insisted on their taking morning and afternoon strolls, saying the fresh air would speed his recovery. Preacher didn't argue. He listened to her talk about her father, her tribe, and the beauty of the natural wonders around them. She displayed an abiding faith in the Spirit, the Everywhere Spirit as he understood it. She didn't pry into his past, and for that he was grateful.

Preacher was elated to discover Red Echo had retrieved his horse. The chestnut stallion was being well tended, fed and watered regularly. Preacher's saddle and bedroll, with the .58 caliber inside, was stored under a buffalo robe outside of Red Echo's tipi.

On the evening of the third day, Preacher asked Wallowa to find Red Echo. While he awaited their coming, he donned his white shirt. He had been using a blanket to cover himself while outdoors. His left shoulder was stiff, but mobility wasn't impaired.

Moccasins shuffled on the grass outside, and a moment later Wallowa and Red Echo entered.

Preacher got straight to the point. "I must be leaving tomorrow at sunup. I wish I could stay longer, but I can't. You saved my life, Red Echo. I hope we meet again, some day, so I can pay my debt proper. But what value can you place on your life?" He picked up the Barnes .50 caliber. "This isn't much. Consider it a small token of my esteem. I have ammunition for it in my saddlebags, and the ammunition is yours too. What do you say? Will you honor me by accepting this gift?"

Wallowa translated. Red Echo studied Preacher's face,

# SLAUGHTER AT TEN SLEEP

then the gun. He appeared flattered by the offer. Turning, he briefly addressed Wallowa.

"Red Echo says not necessary," Wallowa said.

"I want to do it," Preacher stated. "Tell him I'll be shamed if he refuses to accept my gift."

Wallowa conveyed the message.

Red Echo nodded his understanding and smiled. He took the Barnes and held it up, obvioiusly delighted.

"Tell him I'll teach him how to shoot it tomorrow morning," Preacher said.

Red Echo departed the tipi beaming like a four-year-old with a new toy.

"Thank you," Wallowa said sincerely.

"Least I could do," Preacher declared, and he meant it.

Wallowa moved closer to Preacher. "Preacher, do something for Wallowa?"

Preacher nodded. "Anything you want, you get. I figure I owe you my life as much as your father."

Wallowa inched nearer. She reached up and gently stroked his right cheek.

Preacher's eyes narrowed.

Wallowa looked down. "Wallowa hungry, Preacher. Hard times after George Wheeler killed. Nez Perce braves not want. You savvy, Preacher?"

Preacher nodded.

Wallowa moved to the tipi entrance and lowered the front flaps. She crossed to Preacher and knelt in front of him, her doelike eyes fastened on his.

Preacher kissed her, lightly at first, but with increasing urgency as their passion mounted. He nibbled on her ears and licked her neck. His hands roamed over her body, removing her clothing. He massaged her taut breasts, tweaking her erect nipples.

Wallowa squirmed and moaned.

Preacher slid his right hand between her legs, touching her moistness, his fingers finding her receptive to his touch. He inserted his middle finger, and she groaned and bit his neck.

Wallowa ground her hips against his, arousing him more.

Preacher laid her on the buffalo robe and parted her silky thighs. She stretched to accommodate his hugeness, sighing as he slipped inside of her. Preacher locked his lips on hers, their tongues entwining. Her natural scent filled his nostrils.

Wallowa was quivering with desire.

Preacher went slowly, moving his organ in and out, savoring the experience. He wanted to make her happy, to return the kindness she had demontrated toward him.

Wallowa ran her nails down his back.

Preacher bent lower, his lips rolling her nipples around and around.

"Yes! Yes, Preacher!" Wallowa cried in a small voice.

Preacher increased his pace. She licked his face and sucked on his lips and eyelids. He placed his hands on her buttocks, holding her steady, and rammed away for all he was worth.

"Ahhh!" Wallowa exclaimed, her head tossing from side to side. She added a string of words in the Nez Perce tongue.

Preacher was breathing heavily and pumping his legs in a rocking motion.

Wallowa arched her back, her eyes fluttering. "Yes! Oh, yes! Do . . ." She gasped, lost in her sexual rapture.

Preacher's arms became corded bands as he discharged. He trembled, racked by the sheer ecstasy. Their sweaty bodies heaved and bucked, straining against one another, their lust consuming them as they climaxed.

"Oh! Oh!" Wallowa uttered a protracted moan.

Preacher collapsed onto her, and they stayed that way for what seemed like forever. Both dozed. They awoke late at night and repeated their performance, then fell asleep.

Preacher awoke first. He quietly dressed while Wallowa slept. He paused at the tipi entrance, gazing at her angelic features. A twinge of regret flitted through his mind. He didn't want to leave her, but he had no choice. Frowning, he crept from the tipi.

Red Echo was waiting for him. The chestnut stallion was properly saddled. True to his word, Preacher gave Red Echo the ammunition for the Barnes .50 caliber. He demonstrated the loading and unloading procedure, and the Nez Perce nodded his understanding. Preacher mounted. He nodded at Red Echo, then cast a wistful look at Wallowa's tipi.

Red Echo glanced from the white man to the tipi, sadness in his eyes.

Preacher wheeled his horse and raced off.
Red Echo watched until the dust from the chestnut stallion's passing had faded in the distance.

# 11

"We're there!" Port exclaimed happily.

Elizabeth stared at the ramshackle cabin and crude corral below them. They were on a ridge covered with buffalo grass. The cabin and corral were in a small valley, not more than a quarter of a mile in length and several hundred yards wide. A placid stream meandered past the cabin and flowed out the south end of the valley. Ridges to the east, north, and west effectively hid the cabin from potential enemies.

Sherm started down the ridge, the others following.

Elizabeth pulled in behind Burt. She was becoming increasingly worried about Sherm. After several days of treating her courteously and hovering over her like a hawk, he seemed to become annoyed because she wasn't responding to his kindness. He stopped talking to her, and became sullen and morose. She noticed his brothers went out of their way to avoid angering him.

Three days after they had abandoned the wagon, they'd spotted a group of Indians on the northern horizon. They'd promptly taken cover in a dry wash, and remained there for the rest of the day. Satisfied the Indians hadn't seen them and weren't lurking nearby, they'd continued their journey the next morning, always bearing to the northwest.

Once, while resting in a stand of trees, some buffalo hunters passed, three white men and an Indian, riding to the southeast with several pack horses loaded with hides. The Bascombs had their hands on their guns the whole while, but the buffalo hunters had kept going, evidently unaware they were being observed.

Two days after the incident with the Indians, they'd stopped in a ravine and spent the entire day arguing. Elizabeth wasn't privy to the reason for their spat. One of them would guard her while the rest moved out of hearing range and debated the cause of their contention. For once, the other brothers seemed to be standing up to Sherm over something. Boone and Burt, in particular, wouldn't back down. The next day the argument resumed, and it wasn't settled until the sun was directly overhead.

Cy mounted up and rode off to the north. The other Bascombs had resumed their northwesterly travel, but the further they went, the more devious their route became. They'd taken to trying to cover their tracks and confusing their trail. They backtracked and circled, then circled again. All of this crafty maneuvering took up considerable time, and two more days had elapsed before they reached the ridge above the cabin and corral.

Now, as she followed Burt toward the cabin, she fretted over her predicament and resolved to do something about it. She'd expected her father to have the cavalry on the kidnapper's heels within hours of her abduction, but as the hours lengthened into days, and the days into an entire week, her spirits flagged, her determination weakened. She couldn't comprehend why her father failed to save her. Sure, she knew he might be unwilling to expose her to harm from the kidnappers. But her father had always been her idol, in a sense, more so even than her mother. General Nels Demming had always impressed her as a man of indomitable will and courageous action. His apparent failure, when it counted the most, devastated her.

The cabin door opened as the Bascombs and their captive approached.

"Pa!" Burt yelled and waved.

Elizabeth's eyes widened.

If Port Bascomb was bearlike, resembling a big, hulking black bear, then their father was a giant grizzly. He stood almost seven feet tall, and there wasn't an ounce of fat on his body. Grinning, he strolled toward them. He wore black pants and boots, and a brown homespun shirt with holes in it. Strapped around his waist, high on his left hip, butt forward, was a Remington New Model Army .44. On his right hip was an Arkansas toothpick in a leather sheath. He wore a crumpled Confederate officer's hat. His face was hidden by a bushy black beard. His eyes were dark, flat.

"Where y'all been? I expected y'all back two days ago."

"Indians and such," Sherm said, dismounting at the small corral.

"Where's your brother Cy?" their Pa asked. "And Rafe and Rufus?"

"They're all off watchin' the blue bellies," Sherm lied.

The Bascomb patriarch stared at Elizabeth. He walked up to her and offered his right hand. "Howdy, ma'am. Pleased to make your acquaintance. I'm Ira Bascomb. Have my boys treated you proper?"

Elizabeth took his hand and slid from her mount. She deliberately glanced at Sherm, then at Ira. "Mostly," she said.

The implication was not lost on Ira. He frowned, then glanced at Burt. "Burt! Inside! Now!"

Burt cringed as he hastened inside the cabin. Ira followed him and the door slammed.

"Now you're goin' to get it!" Port said, looking at Sherm.

All of the brothers were dismounted. Boone tended to putting their horses in the corral. "I warned you this would happen, Sherm," he said over his shoulder.

Sherm, clearly nervous, was watching the cabin door. "He'd best not, is all I got to say!"

"Oh, yeah? What are you goin' to do?" Port demanded. "Pull on Pa?"

Boone joined them. "You try that, and I'll kill you myself, Sherm."

Elizabeth was confused, at a loss to explain what was transpiring.

A minute elapsed.

The cabin door flew open and Ira Bascomb stalked outside. Burt dangled from his huge right fist.

"I had to tell 'im," Burt wailed at Sherm. "He made me!"

Ira released Burt, who sprawled onto the ground.

"I won't stand for it!" Sherm said to his father.

Ira's eyes became feral slits. "Oh, you won't, eh?" He

slowly walked toward Sherm.

Sherm swallowed hard.

"Seems to me you're gettin' a mite big for your britches," Ira said to Sherm.

"I'm a man now!" Sherm declared defiantly. His hands hovered near his Colts.

"A man? A man?" Ira threw back his head and roared. "Is that what you are?"

"Yes!" Sherm responded.

Ira stopped two feet from Sherm. He placed his hands on his hips. "I want to tell you somethin', boy, and you listen good! So you think you're a man? Why? 'Cause you can unlimber them Colts faster than most men? Does that make you a man?"

"It helps!" Sherm replied. "At least I ain't no yellow belly!"

"True," Ira agreed. "But you're a dumb boy. As stupid as they come! And you show no sign of gettin' any smarter! All you ever care about is swingin' a wide loop! You're too quick on the trigger for your own good!" He paused. "I've tried to teach you, Sherm, I truly have. There's more to life than shootin' irons and she-stuff. I know. I rode with Quantrill, up 'till the Kansas massacre. I didn't cotton to killin' women and children, and I still don't."

He pointed at Elizabeth. "Usin' the lady to get the gold was my idea. I couldn't ride with you 'cause I might of been recognized by the Yankee scum around Fort Laramie. But I told you what to do, didn't I?"

"Yes," Sherm responded.

"I told you she wasn't to be touched, didn't I?" Ira asked, his tone deceptively tranquil.

"Yes," Sherm said meekly.

Ira Bascomb could move incredibly quick when he wanted. He took one short step and grabbed Sherm by the front of his shirt. Before Sherm could hope to react, Ira backhanded him once, twice, and a third time, all across the mouth. He shoved Sherm to the ground and towered above him. "So where do you get off tryin' to talk your brothers into lettin' you have her? Where do you get off opposin' your own Pa?"

Sherm was sitting in the dirt, his left hand over his bloody mouth.

Insight dawned. Elizabeth understood the reason for the protracted argument the brothers had become embroiled in on the way to the cabin. Sherm had wanted to bed her, and the others had stood up for her! Or had they?

"Your brothers knew better than to cross me," Ira raged. "At least they don't have rocks in their heads! What would have happened if you'd had your way? Ever think of that?"

Sherm shook his head.

"Course not! All you could think of was yourself! But if you'd laid a hand on her, our deal with the general wouldn't of been worth shucks! And what do you reckon the general would do, once he knew you'd indulged yourself? You dumb polecat! The general would hunt us down from now 'till eternity, if that's what it took!"

Ira stopped, out of steam, his anger spent. He reached down and lifted Sherm to his feet. Then, surprisingly, he hugged his son. "I worry 'bout you boy, I truly do. I suppose it's my own fault. I should of taken you to a Bible-puncher more regular, like your Ma wanted." He released Sherm and stepped back. "You all right?"

Sherm nodded.

"You sure?" Ira persisted.

Sherm wiped blood from his split lower lip. "I'm fine, Pa."

"Good." Ira smiled, then hauled off and backhanded Sherm one more time.

Sherm was knocked to the ground. He looked up at his father in stunned disbelief. "What was that for?"

"For lettin' Rafe and Rufus ride into Cheyenne alone!" Ira yelled. "Them boys ain't got the brains God gave a turnip! And you ain't much better! If Rafe and Rufus don't get back here within four days, you're goin' after 'em! You got me?"

Sherm nodded and stood. He glared at Burt, then Elizabeth, then wheeled and walked from view toward the rear of the cabin.

Ira moved over to Elizabeth. "Come on in, Miss Demming. I'll try and make you as comfortable as I can, but the accommodations ain't much to boast of." He waved her toward the front door.

Elizabeth entered the cabin. Ira hadn't exaggerated. The furniture in the one room cabin consisted of a wooden table with four chairs. That was it. Blankets were piled on the hard floor to serve as beds. Two windows, both with the glass panes missing, afforded illumination in the daytime. A lantern rested on the table.

"We fix our vittles outside mostly," Ira said from behind her. "You're welcome to help yourself, even do the cookin' if you like. There's plenty of game hereabouts, and we've got some canned goods too. A few cans of peaches and plenty of Mexican strawberries."

"Do you have a place where a lady can tend to personal matters without being interrupted?" Elizabeth asked sweetly.

Ira shook his head, his beard swaying. "No. Sorry. This place ain't much to look at, but it was worse when we found it. We've actually improved on it some. But we've been too busy to attend to luxuries like an outhouse."

Elizabeth sighed.

"There's thick bushes yonder," Ira said, stepping to the doorway and pointing to the east. "If you hunker down, no one will be the wiser."

"Thank you." Elizabeth moved past Ira and started toward a dense growth of sage.

"You want one of my boys to keep a watch?" Ira called out.

"Thank you, but no," Elizabeth replied over her left shoulder. "I can manage."

"You see any Injuns or snakes, you give a yell, hear?" Ira advised her.

Elizabeth reached the sage, about twenty yards from the cabin, and ducked from view. She peered through an opening in the vegetation at the cabin and corral, waiting. She'd lied. She didn't need to tend to business. She planned to escape. The minutes dragged by. Ira came to the door once and gazed in her direction, then went inside. Finally, what she'd been waiting for! Sherm appeared at the west side of the cabin and walked inside.

Elizabeth jumped up and ran toward the rear of the building. The two windows were located on the front, one on either side of the front door, the only door. If she could put the cabin between the Bascombs and herself, she might be able to reach the corral and steal a horse. She had no idea where she was, but she didn't intend to stay with the Bascombs another day! If her father couldn't see fit to come to her rescue, then she'd just have to save herself.

None of the Bascombs were in sight.

Elizabeth reached the east side of the cabin, then crept around the rear. The corral was on the west side. She ran to the northwest corner and risked a peek.

The horses were resting in the corral. One of them, the lively mare belonging to Sherm, the horse called Belle, was still saddled.

Elizabeth climbed over the rickety fence. She shushed the horses, and swiftly moved to the gate.

Still no sign of the Bascombs.

Elizabeth quietly opened the gate, then ran to Belle. The mare shied for a moment, but settled down when she whispered its name. Elizabeth got aboard. She rode to the gate, moving slowly, hoping the way was still clear.

It was.

Elizabeth goaded Belle forward, breaking into a gallop. She headed south, along the stream, then wheeled and raced up the east ridge.

Behind her, shouts sounded. Yells and curses, but no shots. The Bascombs wouldn't risk harming their barter.

Elizabeth gave the black mare its lead. They raced like the wind across the prairie. Sherm had bragged about Belle, claimed she was the fastest thing on four legs. Maybe she was. The mare ate up the distance with consummate ease.

What about the Bascombs?

Elizabeth glanced over her right shoulder.

The Bascombs were in hot pursuit, every one of them. Sherm, on one of the team animals, was way to the rear, undoubtedly furious as all get out. Then came Port, then Ira on a massive brown stallion. Burt was about two-hundred yards behind her. But the closest, and coming on strong, was Boone Bascomb on his black stallion. The man and horse seemed as one.

Elizabeth knew her only threat was from Boone Bascomb. Ira, Port, and Sherm were too far behind to even begin to catch up. Burt was riding well, but his horse didn't appear as powerful as that black stallion of Boone's.

The landscape flashed by. Over hills, down gullies, up one side and down the other. Then straight stretches, miles at a time. All of the mounts were slowing. Ten miles from the cabin, only Boone Bascomb was still behind her, his black stallion maintaining a steady gait.

So was the black mare. Elizabeth realized it was an endurance test now. Which animal had more stamina? The mare or the stallion? Her hopes and prayers were with the mare, and she stayed alert for ruts and praire dog towns with their treacherous holes. One misstep, any mistake at this speed, and the mare could easily break a leg.

Belle pounded down one side of a steep ravine, then plowed up the other, loose dirt and tiny stones flying in every direction. Elizabeth could feel the animal's sides heaving against her legs. A ragged boulder appeared directly ahead, at the top of the ridge. Elizabeth angled to the right, bypassing the boulder, and found herself on a level plain. She urged Belle onward. The mare, game to the challenge, flew slightly faster.

What about Boone?

Elizabeth looked over her left shoulder.

Boone Bascomb and his black stallion were just coming over the top of the ridge. But something was wrong. The stallion was desperately striving to find its footing, but the unstable earth forming the lip of the ridge gave way. The black stallion reared, and both horse and rider plunged from view.

Elizabeth grinned and faced forward. What a break! Boone would need a minute or two to recover, to get his mount to the top of the ridge again. And every second counted! She squinted, studying the landscape ahead, and her eyes alighted on an unbelievable sight to her left.

A town!

Elizabeth made for the cluster of buildings visible on the horizon. She could distinguish eight or ten structures. It was probably a small settlement. All she had to do was reach it, and she would be safe!

Belle was beginning to show signs of fatigue. The mare slowed slightly, breathing laboriously.

Elizabeth peered over her left shoulder again.

Boone Bascomb had cleared the ridge! The black stallion was sweeping after her, its long mane flying.

Elizabeth stared at the town, gritting her teeth from the tension. Boone had lost ground. He was now over four-hundred yards behind her, which meant she would reach the settlement well before him. If he was smart, and

Boone had given every indication of being one of the smarter Bascombs, he would give up the chase. It had to be obvious to him that she would easily reach the town before he could overtake her. She looked back.

Oddly enough, Boone wasn't dropping off. The black stallion was still coming on strong.

Did Boone intend to follow her into the settlement? Elizabeth wondered. If he did, then he wasn't any smarter than the others. The people in the settlement would protect her. Molesting or harming a woman was one of the vilest acts a man could commit. The townspeople would spring to her defense.

Confident in her imminent deliverance, Elizabeth raced toward the buildings.

Four-hundred yards to her rear, the black stallion galloped after the mare.

# 12

The rotten blue bellies!

Cy Bascomb hated Yankees. He had lost a lot of kinfolk during the war. Cousins. In-laws. Even two uncles and one aunt. Another uncle, his favorite, Uncle Andy, had been gunned down shortly after the war. Bitter times and bitter memories. And Cy blamed all of it on the damn Yankees. If the Northern scum had left well enough alone, Cy's relatives would still be alive. But as Uncle Andy had often said, the North wanted to dictate Southern morality, and where did the North get off casting the first stone? Cy had been mightily stirred by Uncle Andy's eloquence, although he never had understood the stone business.

Now, as he spied on General Demming's soldiers from the canyon wall to their south, it took all of Cy's limited self control to refrain from shooting a few of them. Cy had been surprised to find Demming already on the scene, scouring Ten Sleep Canyon for the stash of gold bars. Cy realized the general must have made a forced march from Fort Laramie with his troops. He snickered as he watched the blue bellies toiling in the hot sun.

Cy had been spying on the Yankees for over a day. An outcropping of rock behind him sheltered him from the sun. There was a stream several hundred yards to the east, with plenty of grass nearby for his brown mare. He'd packed extra grub in his saddlebags to tide him over, including a half dozen cans of love apples.

The Yankees were turning over every stone, and checking every nook and cranny in Ten Sleep Canyon.

Cy chuckled. His Pa had been right, as always. The blue bellies would find the gold a lot quicker than his family could. He felt his stomach grumble and decided to treat himself. Easing from the edge of the canyon wall, so as not to expose himself to the soldiers below, he moved back ten feet, then stood and walked to his mare. He wished he had one of those fancy telescopes or spy glasses, although he didn't really need one. When they found the gold, the Yankees would undoubtedly create enough commotion to rouse the dead!

A warm breeze was blowing in from the southwest.

Cy rummaged through his saddle pockets and found one of the cans containing the love apples. He grinned as he applied his knife to the top of the can. In a minute, the tin was peeled off, exposing the juicy tomatoes inside. He set his knife on the ground, and used his fingers to scoop out a handful of tomatoes. Greedily slurping and smacking, he crammed the food into his mouth.

"I like a man with good table manners," said a deep male voice coming from Cy's left.

Cy tensed and spun, his right hand coated with tomatoes, two of his fingers in his gaping mouth.

A stranger stood about the ten-feet away. A man dressed in black, with a white shirt and a broad brimmed, shallow topped black hat. A nickel plated forty-four forty was held low in his right hand. "You so much as blink," the stranger warned, "and those love apples will be the last food you ever eat."

Cy had been around. He'd hobnobbed with hardcases, with gunmen and gamblers and assorted killers all of his adult life. He knew a deadly gunhand when he saw one, and this particular hombre intuitively impressed him as being a top notch gunslinger.

"I want you to unlimber your hardware," the stranger directed. "Keep your right hand in your mouth. Use your left hand. Thumb and first finger only. Do it!"

Cy complied, tomatoes and red juice dribbling over his chin. He carefully separated his iron from its scabbard, then slowly lowered the Colt to the ground.

"Step back from the iron," the stranger ordered.

Cy did.

"Turn around," the stranger commanded.

Cy immediately obeyed.

"Down on your knees."

Cy dropped to his knees, chafing his left knee on a pointed stone.

"Don't be getting no wild notions," the man in black said. "I'd as soon kill you as keep you alive."

Cy's brain was racing. Why had the gunslinger waylaid him? Robbery? That hardly seemed likely, given the man in black wore finer clothes than Cy. Then why?

"Take your fingers out of your mouth," the stranger instructed.

Cy lowered his right hand, the juice from the tomatoes feeling sticky on his fingers.

"What's your name?" the man in black asked.

"Cy."

"Well, Cy, I'm J. D. Preacher."

Cy's mouth dropped. "The Widah Maker?"

"So they say," Preacher said.

Cy was flabbergasted. He'd heard all about the Widow Maker. Few residents of the frontier hadn't. To cap it off, Cy's family entertained a special interest in the activities of J.D. Preacher. They owed him.

"Where is the girl being held?" Preacher inquired.

"What girl?" Cy responded innocently.

The next moment, the barrel of a forty-four forty pressed against the back of his head.

"You think you're dealing with a tinhorn here, Cy?" Preacher prodded him.

"I sure ain't," Cy replied. "And that's a fact."

"So where's the girl?" Preacher asked. "I know you and your brothers kidnapped General Demming's daughter."

"How do you figure?" Cy responded.

"Your brother, Sherm, had a long talk with General Demming," Preacher said. "Spilt the beans about how his brothers were going to kill her if the general tried anything. I knew you boys would be posting a lookout. All I had to do was search the canyon rim near the soldiers, checking every hiding place, and I knew I'd find myself a snake-headed woman-stealin' polecat."

"Right slick of you," Cy conceded.

"I'm going to ask you one last time," Preacher said. "Where are they keeping the Demming girl?"

"In a cabin 'bout twenty miles west of here," Cy disclosed. He didn't figure the information was worth dying over. Besides, he wasn't dead yet. And the tables could turn any time.

"You're going to take me to it," Preacher said.

"Whatever you want, Mister Preacher," Cy said.

"Stand up."

Cy rose.

"Walk to your horse and get aboard, real slow." Preacher waited while Cy mounted, then wagged his revolver to the left. "Thataway. I'll be right behind you."

Preacher mounted his horse, the barrel of his forty-four forty never wavering from Cy. "Ride out."

Cy headed west.

Preacher holstered his forty-four forty and followed. He didn't trust the surly looking character in front of him, but he knew Cy was unarmed and helpless. Preacher had become adept over the years at spotting hideouts, and Cy didn't have one.

For his part, Cy was annoyed with himself. He'd allowed Preacher to surprise him and disarm him. Behaved like a regular greenhorn. The thought of his Colt reminded him. "Preacher!" he called back.

"Speak your piece."

"What 'bout my gun? We left it lyin' back there," Cy said.

"I don't have any use for it," Preacher said.

"But it's my hogleg!" Cy protested.

"Tell you what," Preacher stated. "If you live, you can go back and claim it."

Cy fell silent. He vowed to get revenge on Mister-High-and-Mighty J.D. Preacher the first chance he got.

Time passed.

Preacher and his prisoner bore ever westward. At one point, Cy started to loop to the south.

"Hold on!" Preacher snapped.

Cy reined in.

"What do you think you're doing?" Preacher demanded. "You said the cabin was due west. Why are you heading south?"

Cy nodded to the west. "Ten Sleep is up ahead. I was figurin' on goin' around, 'less you'd rather go through."

"We'll go around," Preacher said. He didn't want anyone in Ten Sleep to know he was in the area. They might alert Cy's brothers. He didn't want them forewarned of his presence. He could hardly deal with them and Elizabeth Demming's kidnappers at the same time.

Preacher stayed behind Cy's mare as they continued their trip.

"Cy," Preacher said, "need to ask you a question."

"Whatever you want. You've got the drop on me."

"You familiar with most of the families hereabouts?" Preacher asked.

"I reckon most of 'em," Cy answered.

"Ever hear of a family called Bascomb?"

Cy was fortunate Preacher was to his rear, otherwise the bounty hunter would have noticed the completely stupefied expression on Cy's face.

"I asked you if you ever heard of the Bascombs?" Preacher repeated when Cy didn't respond.

Cy finally found his voice. "No. Can't say as I have."

"What's your last name?" Preacher queried.

Cy blurted the first name which popped into his head. "Hickok."

"Hickok?" Preacher said. "You wouldn't be lying to me, would you?" he asked suspiciously.

"Never," Cy replied.

"You any relation to Wild Bill?" Preacher asked.

"Not that I know of," Cy said. "Wild Bill isn't the only man with the handle 'Hickok,' you know."

"I'm pleased to hear you're not related," Preacher stated.

"Oh? Why?"

"Because Jim Hickok and I are friends," Preacher responded. "I wouldn't want to think I was going to kill some of his kin."

Cy grinned, elated by his brilliant deception. This Widow Maker isn't such a tough hombre, after all.

For over three hours they rode in silence, Cy pondering how he could dry gulch the Preacher man, while Preacher deliberated his strategy for when they arrived at the cabin.

Cy stopped at the bottom of the ridge. "Our cabin's on the

other side," he said.

"You first," Preacher stated.

Cy started up the ridge.

Preacher glanced at the ground, discovering a lot of recent tracks. Some went up. Some down. Evidence of an awful lot of activity. He tailed Cy to the top of the ridge, insuring he stayed slightly to Cy's right, putting Cy and the mare between himself and any occupants of the cabin. If the cabin was even there.

It was.

Preacher rose on his stirrups, scanning the scene below. There was one miserable looking cabin and a corral. Three horses were in the corral, but there was no sign whatsoever of any of the kidnappers or the Demming girl. He glanced at Cy, his eyes narrowing.

Cy noticed. "I swear! That's our cabin! I don't know where they got to! Honest!"

Preacher motioned toward the cabin. "Move out."

They reached the bottom of the ridge without mishap. The nearer they grew to the cabin, the more certain Preacher became it was unoccupied. Confirmation was provided by the confused expression on Cy's face; the hawknosed man had obviously expected to find his kin here.

"Climb down," Preacher directed.

Cy dismounted, and as his right hand brushed against the saddlebag on the off side of the mare, his fingers gripped the ring on his picket pin and he pulled the pin free.

Preacher, intently scanning the cabin and corral, hadn't noticed.

Cy smirked. The picket pin was sharp enough to puncture any man, and thick enough to restrain a horse. If he could plunge the pin into Preacher's exposed neck or face, he'd become the family hero for avenging Uncle Andy.

Preacher slid to the ground. He cautiously walked to the cabin door and kicked it open. Satisfied it was empty, he moved to the corral and scrutinized the three horses. Team horses, they appeared to be. They were a little too hefty to be riding animals. He frowned. Where were the kidnappers? Why would they ride off and leave three horses behind? Had they seen Cy and him coming from a distance and elected to tail out, to take it on the run? Immersed in his speculation, Preacher momentarily forgot about Cy Hickok.

He perceived his mistake when he heard gravel crunch behind him.

Preacher spun, pulling his hip gun, relying on his catlike reflexes to stop Cy dead.

Cy had other ideas. As the man in black whirled, Cy tossed the handful of dirt he'd scooped up from near the mare directly into Preacher's eyes.

Preacher still got his shot off, but then the dirt was in his eyes, stinging them like the dickens, burning, causing them to water. He backed up, rubbing his left sleeve across his face, attempting to clear his vision, excpecting Cy to pounce on him at any moment. Although his eyes were still watering, his sight returned after a few swipes with his sleeve.

Cy was lying on the ground five-feet away, doubled over, clutching his abdomen. He wasn't moving.

Preacher wondered if he'd gut shot the bastard. He walked over to the prone figure and nudged Cy's shoulder with his right boot.

Cy whipped around, his legs catching Preacher across the shins and knocking Preacher onto his back.

Preacher's head struck a rock, jarring him, and in the instant he required to recover, Cy was up and on him, trying to bury a picket pin in his neck. Preacher deflected the blow with a swipe of his right arm, and Cy gripped his right wrist before he could straighten it and fire. Holding on to Preacher's right wrist with his left hand, Cy stabbed again and again with the picket pin. Preacher blocked the pin with his left arm. Once, the point of the pin scraped his cheek.

Cy went berserk, gouging and slashing.

Preacher strained, arching his back, and succeeded in flipping them to the right.

Cy held on to Preacher's right wrist for dear life, knowing if the man in black freed his gun hand, he was doomed.

Preacher knew Cy was concentrating on his right hand. Cy naturally expected Preacher to make a herculean effort to wrest his arm loose. But Preacher had learned a valuable lesson years ago. When in a fight to the death, doing the expected was inevitably fatal. Doing the unexpected, however, often assured victory. So Preacher now did exactly that. Cy, his eyes on Preacher's forty-four forty, never saw Preacher's left hand swoop to the small of his back and flash out with the Bowie knife. The Bowie gleamed in the sunlight for an instant, and then its huge blade rammed up and in, slicing into Cy's neck, into his throat, all the way to the hilt.

Cy stiffened, his eyes widening, releasing his grip on Preacher's right wrist. His mouth opened and he wheezed a great gasping sound, as if he was trying to suck all the air of the Wyoming Territory into his mouth at once.

Preacher wrenched the knife from Cy's neck and stood. Blood poured from the gaping hole in Cy's throat. Preacher holstered his forty-four forty. He wiped the Bowie blade clean on Cy's shirt, then sheathed the knife. It had been close. Too close. Preacher couldn't believe he'd missed Cy with his shot. He knelt and examined Cy's stomach, finding the spot three inches above Cy's navel where the bullet had entered.

Cy was gurgling and groaning.

Preacher rose. So his hurried shot had hit the target, just a mite low. Cy must have been strong as a bull to keep battling with his innards blown open.

Cy's mouth was moving, but nothing came out except blood. His right hand feebly motioned toward Preacher.

Preacher knew the man would die a slow, painful, lingering death. And there wasn't any call for it. Preacher had once blown a man's legs off, then cut out his larynx with the Bowie, and left the man alive to suffer an agony of despair for the remainder of the son of a bitch's miserable life. But that had been Christopher Langdon Bowdry, the man responsible for brutally killing his sister Abigail. Cy whatever-his-name-was had never done Preacher any personal harm. The affair between them had been strictly business. Bounty hunter to outlaw. So as a bounty hunter, Preacher opted to do the same thing he would do for a critically injured horse or steer.

Preacher pulled his vest gun and shot Cy smack between the eyes.

# 13

She made it!

Elizabeth Demming could feel her heart pounding as Belle raced into the settlement. She saw people all around her; men, a few women, even several children. Most gawked at her as she thundered into view. Elizabeth had a brief glimpse of a livery, the inevitable saloon, a general store and other buildings, and then she was abreast of a tall man in a black hat.

"Help!" she cried. "I need help!"

Some of the men came running.

"Good Gawd, woman!" yelled the man in the hat. "What are you so all fired agitated 'bout?"

"Some men are after me!" Elizabeth shouted. "I need help!"

"Who's after you, miss?" a burly man demanded. "We'll take care of 'em!"

"They're right behind me!" Elizabeth told them. "They're called the Bascombs!"

That did the trick. Every man within hearing promptly vanished. So did the women and children. Within the space of a minute, Elizabeth was the only person still on the only street in the settlement.

"Wait!" she shouted. "I need your help!"

No one responded. Doors and windows were closing right

and left. Somewhere, in a nearby house, a child wailed.

Elizabeth glanced over her shoulder. Boone Bascomb wasn't in sight yet, but he would be any second. She dropped from Belle and ran to a frame structure to her left. The door was shut, and she pounded on the wood with all her strength.

"Help me!"

No one came to the door.

Desperate, on the verge of hysteria, Elizabeth ran to the next building in line, the general store. The door was open. She dashed inside, scarcely noticing the shelves of merchandise on display. She saw a tall woman standing behind a counter and ran over.

"Please! I need help!"

"So I gathered," the woman replied. She was in her forties, but had retained her shape well. Red hair flowed over her shoulders. Frank green eyes appraised the trembling girl. Her green dress complimented her eyes nicely.

"Didn't you hear me?" Elizabeth cried. "I need help!"

"Honey," the woman responded. "They could hear you clear to Cheyenne."

"The Bascombs are after me!" Elizabeth shrieked.

"I heard you out in the street," the woman said. "What do you want me to do about it?"

"Help me! Please!"

The woman pursed her red lips and stared at the door. "I know I'll live to regret this, but all right. Follow me, and be quick about it!"

The woman led Elizabeth behind the counter and past a curtain. A short hallway led to a locked door. The woman produced the keys from under a small barrel next to the door.

"Some of the kids used to sneak in here and swipe some of the candy," she explained idly as she unlocked the door. "I couldn't very well let them eat into my profits."

The door swung open.

"Inside," the woman directed.

Elizabeth hesitated.

"Do you want a place to hide or not?" the woman demanded. "I can't guarantee they won't find you here, but it's the only place you're going to find."

Elizabeth stepped into the darkened storage room.

"Keep the lantern out," the woman said. "There's plenty of food to eat if you get hungry. And stay away from the rear window."

The storage room was stocked with jars of sweets, canned food, and dry goods.

"Wait!" Elizabeth said as the woman prepared to close the door. "What's your name?"

"Brooke, honey. Brooke Merriweather. Now you hush and be still. I'll get back as soon as I can."

Brooke closed and locked the door, deposited the key under the barrel, and smiled. She walked to the front of her store and reached the counter just as a tall figure in buckskins entered.

"Brooke!" Boone Bascomb called. He was holding his needle gun in his right hand. It was called a needle gun because of its long needle-like firing pin, it was a Model 1866 Springfield .50-70 Allin conversion. In the right hands, the needle gun was deadly at great distances.

"Boone! What can I do for you?" Brooke replied.

"Lookin' for a sprout of a girl in a white dress," Boone said. "Rode in here but a minute or two ago."

"Was that what all that fuss outside was about?" Brooke asked innocently.

"Yeah. Have you seen her?" Boone queried.

Brooke swept the store with her left hand. "See for yourself. Maybe she's hiding under that pile of men's britches yonder."

Broone frowned. "I ain't got time for funnin', Brooke. If you see her, give a yell. My brothers and Pa will be here in a bit, and we won't be leavin' 'till we find her." He turned and walked away.

Brooke breathed a sigh of relief. The poor girl was safe, for a while at least. She wondered why the Bascombs were after the girl in the storeroom? Whatever the reason was didn't matter. Brooke despised the Bascombs. She hated Ira, Sherm, Cy and Port; disliked the youngest ones, Burt, Rafe, and Rufus; and merely tolerated Boone. Boone was the best of the bunch, which wasn't saying very much. He didn't leer after her and paw her the way the others did.

She'd abided enough pawing to last her a lifetime. From the saloons in Denver to the saloons in Cheyenne, she'd spent many a night with sweaty, stinking range riders running their grimy hands over her body while they praised her beauty and tried to show how manly they could be. She'd tired of the trade eventually, but the years of lying on her back with some man blowing in her ear paid off. She'd accumulated at tidy bankroll, and she used her money to finance the purchase of a general store in a sleepy little community where she would never be pawed again.

Or so she thought.

Ten Sleep had been heaven on earth for the first seven years. It was a quaint settlement inhabited by hard working farmers and aspiring ranchers determined to come out on top in their struggle with the harsh land. She'd been treated courteously. Respected.

And then the damn Bascombs rode into Ten Sleep and everything changed. The Bascombs knew a perfect setup when they saw one. No law to give them trouble. No one with enough backbone to stand up to them. Ira and his boys had taken over an abandoned cabin to the west of Ten Sleep, and their weekly visits served as a study in terror. They mistreated the womenfolk and abused the men. Ira tried to keep a tight rein on his boys when it came to the women, but he couldn't be everywhere at once. Sherm and Cy, in particular, forced themselves on several of the women. The women were too afraid to protest, to fight. Sherm had marched Brooke into the storage room at gunpoint one night, and compelled her to satisfy him.

Right then and there, Brooke had vowed she would get revenge. She didn't know how to go about it, but she knew she would. Sooner or later the Bascombs would make a mistake. She toyed with the notion of leaving Ten Sleep, but she had too much invested in her general store to up and leave. And finding a buyer was impossible because any interested parties invariably learned about the Bascombs prior to finalizing their purchase.

So she was stuck.

Boone Bascomb abruptly appeared in her doorway. He surveyed the interior of the store, then strolled up to the counter. "I'd like a can of those peaches," he said, nodding toward one of the shelves.

"I thought you were looking for some girl," Brooke commented as she moved to the shelf.

"She went to ground," Boone said, "but we'll find her. I'm waitin' on Pa and my brothers. She won't be goin' nowhere. I've locked all the horses in the livery and told old man Jenks to skedaddle until I tell him different."

Brooke took an opener from under the counter. "Sounds to me like you've got this girl boxed in."

"I reckon I do," Boone said, grinning.

Brooke opened the can of peaches and handed it to Boone. "Who is she, anyway? Why are you after her?"

Boone shook his head. "Don't be pokin' your nose in where it don't concern you," he warned.

"I was just asking," Brooke stated defensively.

"Ask Pa when he gets here," Boone suggested. He chuckled and departed.

Brooke leaned on the counter, consciously repressing her anger. Who was that girl? What the hell were the Bascombs up to this time? If the Bascombs wanted her so bad, then they would undoubtedly be extremely upset if she were to escape from Ten Sleep. Here was an opportunity for a little of that revenge. Brooke rested her chin in her hands and studied on how to effect the girl's escape.

# 14

The kidnappers had to return sooner or later.

Preacher had dragged Cy's body behind the cabin and covered it with brush. Next, he'd unsaddled Cy's brown mare and placed the animal in the corral with the three team horses. His horse was a different matter. He couldn't very well leave the stallion in the corral. The kidnappers would be sure to spot an extra animal in with theirs and shy away.

Preacher recalled that the tracks he'd seen on the ridge were all coming or going eastward. Logic dictated the kidnappers would return from the same direction. So he led the stallion to the rear of the cabin and tethered him there, flush against the wall, knowing it was a risk but realizing there was no other choice. The kidnappers might not spot him from the east ridge. Preacher had taken his .58 caliber and entered the cabin.

Now all he could do was wait.

Preacher contemplated riding into Ten Sleep, but decided against the idea. The same reasons he'd avoided Ten Sleep earlier still held true. He settled down to wait, sitting in one of the chairs he'd moved to near the door. This way, he could keep an eye peeled on the east ridge.

The afternoon waned. Evening arrived. The sun was a blazing ember above the western horizon.

His stallion whinnied.

Preacher instantly became alert. Someone was approaching the cabin, and they weren't coming from the east. Preacher crept to the left of the open door, listening.

The horses in the corral were acting skittish.

Preacher heard a distinct footstep from outside the door, to the left. Then a muffled tread to his right. There were two of them, and they were closing in on the door from both sides. He quickly moved around behind the door and crouched, hoping they wouldn't spot him through the narrow crack between the door and the jamb.

A dark form filled the crack, passed it.

Someone was standing in the doorway.

"I told you there's nobody here!" a male voice declared.

Preacher's brow creased. There was something familiar about the voice. He'd heard it before. But where?

"They must have moved on," the man asserted.

"And leave horses?" asked another voice, an older voice with a clipped accent.

"Why not?" demanded the first man.

"Even one saddled in back?" asked the second man.

"There's nobody here, I tell you!" the first man stated impatiently.

Boots pounded on the floorboards.

Preacher leaped from hiding, the .58 leveled, fairly certain who he would find. And he was right.

Lieutenant James froze in the act of replacing his revolver in the flapped holster on his right hip. His eyes widened in astonishment. Behind him, an elderly Indian in buckskins went to raise his Winchester .44 carbine, but thought better of the idea.

"Preacher!" Lieutenant James exclaimed.

Preacher elevated the barrel of the .58. "If I'd been one of the kidnappers you'd be dead right now," he stated disdainfully. "Getting the drop on you is as easy as breathing. Are you trying to get yourself killed?"

Lieutenant James, thoroughly embarrassed, shook his head.

"Tried to tell him," the Indian said. "But what does old Indian know, eh?"

"What are you doing here?" Preacher asked James.

The lieutenant fidgeted as he answered. "I want to help

Beth. So I talked Lone Eagle here into comin' along. He'd been keepin' an eye on the man on the canyon rim for me. When you showed up, I decided to have Lone Eagle track you. I thought you wouldn't mind."

"You figured wrong," Preacher responded testily. "I work alone. I don't need to be dragging deadwood all over creation."

"But I might come in handy!" Lieutenant James protested.

Preacher sighed. "You're going to get yourself killed. And for what? What's between you and Miss Demming?"

"Nothin'," James admitted reluctantly. "But I fell in love with her the moment I saw her. She doesn't even know I exist. She's only spoken to me once or twice at the fort."

Preacher could admire the lieutenant's gumption. But the last thing he needed now was an overzealous junior officer suffering from acute infatuation. He glanced at the Indian. "So you're Lone Eagle? General Demming spoke highly of your tracking skills."

Lone Eagle grinned, adding to the dozens of creases crisscrossing his weathered features. "Old Crow know a little bit about some things, eh?"

He paused, studying Preacher. "You are the man who makes many widows," he stated matter-of-factly.

"You should have known better than to bring him here," Preacher said to the Crow, indicating the lieutenant with a nod of his head.

Lone Eagle nodded. "Little Britches would have come anyway. Needed someone to watch out for him."

"Little Britches?" Preacher repeated.

"That's what Lone Eagle calls me," Lieutenant James said, averting his gaze.

Preacher couldn't help but grin. "Well, Little Britches, you and Lone Eagle had best vamoose. Mosey on back to Ten Sleep Canyon."

Lieutenant James straightened. "No."

"What?"

"No, sir. I aim to see this through to the end," Lieutenant James declared defiantly.

"Does General Demming know you're here?" Preacher asked.

"No," James replied. "I'm doin' this on my own."

"Which means you'll be in a heap of trouble when you return," Preacher deduced. "If you're not already. Do yourself a favor. Leave Beth to me."

"I can't do that," James said.

"You're too stubborn for your own good," Preacher commented.

"I want to tag along with you," James proposed.

"Nope."

"You can't stop me!" Lieutenant James asserted. "If you leave, I'll come after you. The only way you can stop me from helpin' Beth is by killin' me!"

Preacher glanced at Lone Eagle, who made a rolling motion with his brown eyes, then back at Lieutenant James. "I'm not about to waste a bullet on your mangy hide. And I sure as blazes don't want you dogging my trail every step of the way."

James waited expectantly.

"All right," Preacher said at length. "I reckon I'm stuck with you for a spell." He stared into James' blue eyes. "But you listen to me, and you listen good! I'm in charge here! What I say, goes. When I tell you to do something, you'd damn well better do it and be right quick about it! Any objections?"

"No," Lieutenant James responded happily. "I won't get in your way. I promise!"

"If I believed that," Preacher said, "I'd be a bigger fool than you are."

Lone Eagle chuckled.

"Where are your horses?" Preacher questioned the officer.

"On the other side of the west ridge," James disclosed. "We circled all the way around in case anyone was here. Wanted to catch 'em off guard."

"From now on, I'll do the catching," Preacher said. "Go fetch your horses."

"Why can't Lone Eagle do it?" James replied.

Preacher's face hardened. "What did I just get through telling you? I give the orders! Go get your horses!"

Sulking, Lieutenant James exited the cabin.

Lone Eagle waited until James was out of earshot. "Now

you understand why Lone Eagle came? Take care of Little Britches."

"Why fret yourself over him?" Preacher inquired.

"Many years ago," Lone Eagle said, "a white man saved Lone Eagle and Lone Eagle's family from Sioux. The white man was bluecoat. Lone Eagle has been saving bluecoats ever since."

"Sounds to me like you've got your hands full," Preacher remarked.

"Little Britches is good man," Lone Eagle said. "Just young."

"The way he's going," Preacher commented, "your Little Britches isn't going to get much older."

Preacher moved to the doorway and waited. The sun was almost below the western horizon, and darkness was descending. Lieutenant James returned with the horses. Preacher instructed James to place the pair behind the cabin with his. He couldn't predict when the kidnappers might return, and he wasn't taking any chances. Cy's surprise earlier in the day when they'd found the cabin vacant had been genuine. The kidnappers were supposed to have been there. Something important must have caused them to leave. But what?

"Has General Demming come close to finding the gold yet?" Preacher asked the lieutenant.

"No," James replied. "At least he hadn't when I left. They were lookin' under every pebble and behind every bush, but you know how big Ten Sleep Canyon is. They could search for a month of Sundays and still not find it. The Army hunted for it before and failed. I don't expect the general to fare much better."

"Let's hope the kidnappers don't share your confidence," Preacher said.

"Speakin' of the kidnappers," Lieutenant James said, "what happened to the one you were with?"

"He had an appointment he had to keep," Preacher replied.

"An appointment?" Lieutenant James reiterated, puzzled.

"In Hell," Preacher declared.

"Oh. What about the others? Have you seen any sign of 'em? Or Beth?" James asked anxiously.

"I saw a lot of tracks on the east ridge," Preacher revealed. "But I haven't seen hide nor hair of the kidnappers or General Demming's daughter."

"Where the dickens could they be?" Lieutenant James inquired.

"I wish I knew," Preacher stated.

# 15

Brooke Merriweather was pretending to be poring over the account books by lantern light behind the counter in her general store, when actually she was scheming a means of spiriting the girl the Bascombs wanted away from Ten Sleep, when Ira Bascomb and Sherm entered her store.

"Ira," Brooke said by way of a greeting, hoping her face didn't betray her loathing of the man.

Ira walked up to the counter. "Workin' late, Miss Merriweather, aren't you?"

Brooke tapped the account book in front of her. "I'm trying to see if I made two cents or three cents profit this month."

Ira grinned. "Never could see why a woman would want to run a general store. It's a man's work, pure and simple."

Brooke simply plastered a phony grin on her mouth.

"We're havin' a town meetin,' over at the Tiger Saloon," Ira informed her. "Everyone is invited."

"I'm busy with my books," Brooke told him.

Ira placed his huge right hand on top of her account book. "I suppose I didn't explain it proper, Miss Merriweather. Everyone is invited, and we insist on y'all comin'."

Now Brooke understood. It wasn't an invitation. It was an ultimatum.

"Everyone is going to be there?" she asked.

"Yup. My boys are roundin' up the others. Be there in ten minutes," Ira instructed her.

"If you'd like," Sherm piped in, "I'll come fetch you over."

"Thank you. No," Brooke said stiffly. "I can find my way to the Tiger without your assistance."

"Suit yourself," Sherm said, "but you don't know what you're missin'!"

Ira glanced at Sherm. "Didn't those whacks on the head do you any good? You be civil to Miss Merriweather, you hear?"

"Yes, Pa," Sherm said, smirking.

"Let's be on our way," Ira said. He headed for the door. Sherm winked at Brooke, then followed his father.

Brooke watched Sherm close her door. She turned and hastened to the storage room.

"Honey! Can you hear me?" she said, her ear to the door.

"I can hear you," came the reply.

"You need anything?" Brooke inquired.

"No."

"The outhouse?"

"I'm fine," replied the girl.

"Okay. Listen. The Bascombs have been looking all over for you. I know it's dark in there, but I wouldn't risk lighting the lantern. The Bascombs might see the light through the window and come for a looksee," Brooke explained.

"I understand," the girl said.

"You've got grit, honey. I'll give you that." Brooke paused. "I don't have much time. The Bascombs want everyone in the saloon in a few minutes. You be still and wait for me to get back. We'll get you out of this," Brooke assured her.

"Thank you," came the weak reply.

Brooke hurried to the front of the store. Pity welled up in her heart for the poor girl in the storage room. She realized she didn't even know the girl's name yet! Through her window she could see townspeople moving toward the saloon. Ira had been true to his word; it looked like every resident of Ten Sleep, all the men, women and children, were walking to the Tiger.

Brooke grabbed her red shawl from a hook near the door.

She wrapped the cloth around her shoulders, then opened her door and stepped into the cool night.

The Tiger Saloon was located directly across the street from her general store. Its owner, Colin Rennert, had opened the saloon one year before Brooke's arrival in Ten Sleep. Rennert was an over-the-hill gambler. He'd always enjoyed high stakes faro games, and had named his saloon after one of the pet expressions of faro players. Faced by high odds, faro players were considered to be "bucking the tiger" when they played the game. Rennert had even commissioned an artist from Cheyenne to paint a tiger on the sign over the saloon.

Port and Boone Bascomb were standing on the plank walk outside the Tiger Saloon, scrutinizing everyone who entered.

Brooke took a deep breath and made for the saloon, trying to appear as nonchalant as possible.

"Howdy, ma'am," Port greeted her, his hungry eyes measuring her form.

"Brooke," Boone said, nodding and grinning.

"I hope this is important," Brooke said.

"It's just a nice, friendly get together," Port remarked, and cackled.

Brooke went through the black swinging doors. The saloon was more filled than she'd ever seen it. The men were congregating at the bar along the west wall. The women and children sat in the chairs to the gaming tables situated in the eastern half of the establishment. Brooke walked to the nearest chair and sat down.

More townsfolk came into the saloon.

Brooke spotted Burt Bascomb at the north end of the bar, a drink in his left hand. She almost felt sorry for the boy. Under the right influence, he might have amounted to something. As it was, he'd already killed three men and was rapidly becoming as cold-blooded as his older brothers.

Ira and Sherm became visible through the crowd at the south of the bar. Both were drinking.

Brooke saw Sherm's snake-eyes flick in her direction, and she shivered. She prayed he wasn't about to start in on her again! Sherm was the worst Bascomb. He'd gun a man down at the slightest provocation. Gossip had it Sherm had killed fourteen men. To his credit, he'd never backshot anyone.

## SLAUGHTER AT TEN SLEEP

They were all stand-up gun fights. Sherm, so the story went, had shot them all before their iron could clear their scabbard.

Port and Boone sidled inside. They stayed near the entrance, one on either side of the swinging doors. Boone nodded at Ira.

Brooke noticed Boone was carrying his needle gun.

Ira clambered onto the bar and raised his hands. "Quiet down! Quiet down!" he shouted.

The saloon became as quiet as a graveyard.

Ira scanned the people below him. He began counting them, but gave it up when he reached twenty-nine. Ira wasn't much for numbers and usually relied on his fingers.

"I'll make this short and to the point," he declared. "You all know a girl rode lickety-split into town today. And you most likely have heard we're lookin' for her."

"Why do you want her?" asked Colin Rennert, the saloon owner. He was in his fifties, balding, and a natty dresser, wearing a blue pin stripe suit and a black muley, the grandest hat in Ten Sleep.

Ira glared at Rennert. "That's our business," he growled.

"What does it have to do with us?" Rennert inquired.

Brooke sensed a tension in the room. Of everyone present, Colin Rennert was least likely to submit to the Bascombs without an argument. Rennert toted a pistol in a shoulder holster under his left arm, and he wasn't a slouch with the hardware.

"Don't prod me," Ira warned Rennert. He surveyed the crowd. "I want to know where that girl is. She didn't leave Ten Sleep. All the horses have been locked in the livery. And she damn well didn't leave afoot! Which means one of you is hidin' her! Who is it? Speak up now and we'll go easy on you!"

No one spoke.

Ira's jaw muscles twitched. "This ain't the time to be foolin' around! We want her and we'll take this town apart, board by board if we have to, to find her!"

"Like hell you will!" Colin Rennert snapped.

Instantly, everyone was scrambling to put as much distance between Rennert and themselves as possible. Rennert wound up alone, standing near the middle of the bar.

"What did you say?" Ira demanded.

"You won't be touching the Tiger," Rennert said.

"And who's goin' to stop us?" Ira asked.

Rennert's shoulders straightened. "I reckon I am."

"Don't bite off more than you can chew," Ira threatened.

"I've taken all I'm going to take from you Bascombs!" Rennert declared. "You've pushed folks around too long! Why don't you go back to the foul hole in Tennessee you crawled out from!"

Ira's eyes were blazing in fury. He looked at Sherm.

Sherm Bascomb took a few steps to his left, placing himself in a direct line with Colin Rennert. Sherm's thumbs were hooked in the front of his black sash.

Rennert stared up at Ira on the bar. "He doing your dirty work for you?"

Ira grinned and nodded. "The boy can always use the practice."

"That I can," Sherm agreed. His blue eyes locked on Rennert. "I've been lookin' forward to this, Colin. I always figured you for havin' more backbone than anyone else in Ten Sleep. Looks like you proved me right."

Rennert nodded. "I should have done this long ago. In the old days, I never backed down to no man."

"I heard you were a regular curly wolf in the old days," Sherm said. "But these ain't the old days, Colin. And right here and now is where the curly wolf looses his teeth."

Brooke was scarcely breathing. She hadn't witnessed a shooting scrape in ten years. The last time had been at a saloon in Denver, when a drunken farm boy had accused a professional gambler of cheating and went for his hog-leg. The gambler had pulled an over-and-under derringer and shot the farm boy in the forehead. Brooke had been standing to the right of the unfortunate boy, and part of his brains and blood had spattered her dress. She'd hoped she'd never have to see anything like that again.

Colin Rennert made the first move, his right hand streaking to his shoulder holster. Fast as he was, his opponent was faster.

Sherm Bascomb's Navy Colts boomed and bucked.

Rennert was hit in the mouth, both bullets bursting out the rear of his cranium and showering the bar, the floor, and several of the tables with crimson and bits of flesh and skin and hair. His head flipped backwards, and he was propelled about six feet to crash onto his back on top of one of the tables. His arms flopped to the side. He twitched once, then lay still.

Sherm, smiling, spun the Colts, their nickel plating glittering in the lantern light. He eased their barrels under his black sash and sighed. "Just once, Pa, I'd like to meet me some real competition."

Ira chuckled.

None of the townsfolks had moved.

"You see that?" Ira bellowed, pointing at Colin Rennert's body. "You see what happens when you go against the Bascombs? Anyone else want some of Sherm's peas?"

No one uttered a sound.

Ira's chest puffed up. "All right then. Like I was sayin'. We know the girl is still in Ten Sleep. We want her. It's as simple as that. One of you is hidin' her! We'll give you 'till sunrise to hand her over to us! If you don't, we'll make you sorry you were ever born!"

Still none of the townspeople spoke.

"Sunrise!" Ira thundered. He jumped to the floor and strode toward the swinging doors.

Sherm walked after his father.

Burt Bascomb came around the north end of the bar. He paused when he reached Colin Rennert's body, gazing at the dead man's face. Finally he grinned and spat on the body.

"Let's go, Burt!" Ira shouted from the doorway.

Burt ran to join his kin.

The swinging doors swiveled a few times, and the Bascombs were gone.

A collective sigh of relief flooded the saloon. The townsfolk commenced whispering amongst themselves.

Brooke stood and walked to the bar. She stepped behind it and located a bottle of red eye. Oblivious to the incredulous stares of the people around her, she uncapped the bottle and raised it to her lips. The liquid burned as it trickled down her throat, and she almost gagged. As it was, her face flushed and her eyes watered. It had been a long time between drinks.

"Are you ailing, Miss Merriweather?" one of the women

asked.

Brooke set the bottle on the bar. "Never felt better," she said, and made for the door.

The citizens of Ten Sleep took to debating who should remove Colin Rennert's remains.

Brooke reached the swinging doors. She peered into the street, seeking the Bascombs, but they weren't in sight. With her shawl tight, she walked outside, looking in both directions, perplexed because the Bascombs had up and vanished. Strange, she told herself. Where could they be? She glanced at her store, wondering if they were inside.

They weren't.

The large doors to the livery at the west end of Ten Sleep unexpectedly swung wide, and out rode the Bascombs. Ira, Sherm, Boone, Port and Burt seemed to be in a hurry. They galloped off to the south.

Very strange.

Brooke moved to the street, watching the Bascombs disappear into the night. Why were they leaving Ten Sleep? It didn't make sense. The Bascombs should have stuck around, to insure the girl didn't escape. What would make them leave?

A pounding of hooves arrested her attention to the east. The sight she saw caused her to beam with joy.

Four members of the U.S. Army were riding into Ten Sleep from the east!

Brooke started toward them, eager to inform them about the Bascombs, but a wild yell stopped her in her tracks.

One of the soldiers was hollering and waving his arms like crazy. Another one had his revolver in his right hand. He aimed at one of the lanterns hanging on the front porch of a frame house, and squeezed the trigger. The iron cracked, and the lantern exploded in a shower of glass and sparks. A third trooper was tilting a bottle to his mouth.

They were drunk! Brooke turned and ran toward her store.

"Lookee here!" one of the inebriated men in blue shouted. "A fine filly for the taking!" He spurred his horse and cut between the woman in green and the general store.

Brooke stopped and stared up at the soldier. He was young, not much out of his teens. "Please! Let me pass!" she

# SLAUGHTER AT TEN SLEEP

beseeched him.

The young trooper glanced at his three companions. "What do you reckon I should do with her?"

One of the others pointed at the Tiger Salon. "Let's have her over for a drink."

"I don't want a drink!" Brooke stated.

"What's a matter?" asked the youth. "You too good to drink with soldiers?"

"It's not that," Brooke said.

"Then what?" the youth demanded belligerently. "You think all cavalrymen stink like horse sweat, is that it?"

"No," Brooke replied, trying to walk around his mount.

The youth suddenly dropped to the street and grabbed her left wrist. "Come on! Share a drink with us!"

The three other troopers rode up to the front of the Tiger Saloon and dismounted, joking and laughing.

"Leave me be!" Brooke cried, attempting to jerk free.

"You stop that!" the youth scolded her. He yanked on her arm, pulling her after him as he crossed the street and entered the saloon behind his three friends.

All four soldiers abruptly stopped just inside the swinging doors.

"What do we have here?" asked the oldest of the group, a grizzled man with grey muttonchops.

The residents of Ten Sleep seemed to be stupefied by the appearance of the troopers.

"What the hell is this?" demanded the soldier with the muttonchops. "If I didn't know better, I'd swear I was in church 'stead of a saloon!"

The other troopers laughed.

One of the townsmen hurried up to the soldiers. "Thank the Lord you're here!"

"The Lord had nothing to do with it!" muttonchops said, and tittered, weaving on his feet.

"You're drunk!" the townsman declared in surprise.

"We sure as hell are!" muttonchops agreed. "And we aim to get drunker!"

"We need your help," the townsman persisted.

"We ain't here to help!" the trooper barked. "We're here to drink!"

"You don't understand!" the townsman said.

"Out of my way!" The soldier with the muttonchops shoved the bewildered townsman aside.

"Wait!" The townsman took hold of the trooper's shirt "There's been a killing!"

Muttonchops spotted the body of Colin Rennert. "Well, look at this! Some poor bastard went and got himself kilt!"

"These folks must have started to celebrate without us, Dick," the young trooper said to the man with the muttonchops.

"Weren't neighborly of 'em," Dick responded.

"We need your help!" the townsman insisted. "You're soldiers, aren't you?"

Dick reached up and clutched his cap. He snickered and tossed it to the floor. "Not no more we ain't! We didn't sign up to spend our days digging dirt and groping under rocks!"

"Are you going to help us or not?" the irate townsman asked.

"Not," Dick said, and whipped his gun from its holster. He slammed the barrel across the townsman's head, and the hapless citizen dropped to the floor. Dick wagged his iron at the townsfolk. "Get the hell out of here! We want to be alone! If you had a killing, you go find a marshall or a sheriff. But you let us drink in peace, or you'll have more than one killing on your hands!"

Already unnerved by the Bascombs and the death of Colin Rennert, the residents of Ten Sleep required scant incentive to vacate the saloon. They bustled past the four troopers and out the swinging doors without a word.

"Now that's more like it," the soldier named Dick commented when they were alone. "I don't see no barkeep, so let's help ourselves!"

Brooke was hauled toward the bar by the young trooper. She knew she couldn't rely on these soldiers for aid; they were deserters. The Bascombs must have seen the troopers riding in the east end of town and assumed the soldiers were part of a regular cavalry patrol. So the Bascombs had hightailed it out of Ten Sleep, which was good for the girl in the storage room, but bad for Brooke.

"What'll it be?" the young trooper asked her.

"Please. I don't want a drink," Brooke said.

"Dick! This lady says she don't want a drink," the youth declared.

Dick was behind the bar, lifting bottles and examining their labels. He glanced up. "If she won't drink of her own accord Harry, we can help her along."

Harry nodded. His unfocused brown eyes glared at Brooke. "What's it going to be? We can do this easy or hard. Your choice."

With a sinking feeling in her stomach, Brooke realized she had gone from the frying pan into the fire.

# 16

Preacher slipped from the cabin in the middle of the night. Lieutenant James was snoring in the corner. Lone Eagle appeared to be asleep under the table, but Preacher knew the crafty Indian was aware of his departure.

The sky overhead was rampant with stars.

The trio had spent several hours discussing the kidnapping. Lieutenant James had revealed he originally hailed from Kentucky, which explained his slight Southern drawl. James had come west to find fame and fortune, but the austereness of life on the plains had convinced him security and stability were preferable to fleeting fame and fickle fortune, and he'd enlisted. The schooling he'd received in Kentucky served him in good stead in his new career, and he'd risen to the rank of lieutenant in short order.

Preacher had listened to James ramble on. He'd almost laughed aloud when Lieutenant James had bemoaned the hardships he had encountered in his life. Compared to Preacher, Lieutenant James had enjoyed a life of relative ease. A few Indians skirmishes had been the extent of James' fighting experience. The lieutenant was eager to find a wife and settle down, and he'd set his sights on Elizabeth Cole Demming.

Somewhere in the night, a screech owl called.

# SLAUGHTER AT TEN SLEEP

He'd determined to ride into Ten Sleep and look the town over. If the kidnappers were there, riding into the Ten Sleep in broad daylight would only invite trouble. But if he went in at night, when most folks were asleep, he should be able to nose around undetected. Ten Sleep, like every other settlement and town, undoubtedly had a saloon. It was late, but the saloon might still be open, and barkeeps were notorious fountains of information.

A jack rabbit bounded across his path.

Preacher reached the top of the east ridge and headed in the direction of Ten Sleep. Preacher worked alone, so the sooner he ditched James, the better.

A gusty breeze was blowing from the west. Preacher stayed alert for Indians. Once a coyote howled to the north and was answered by one to the south.

Preacher occasionally gazed up at the starry sky, awed by the flickering pinpoints of light. The prairie at night was inspiring.

Ten Sleep eventually materialized on the horizon. Quite a few lanterns were still lit, providing a reference point for travelers.

Preacher cautiously neared the town. He wasn't anticipating trouble, but it paid to play it safe. No one knew he was in the area, nor anything about his mission. He should be able to ride in, scout around, and ride out. Or so he thought.

There was a noise to his right, to the south.

Preacher stopped, peering into the darkness. He saw a buckboard loaded with people bearing to the south. He heard voices; a man, a woman, and children. What was going on here, he asked himself? Who would be taking their family for an outing at this late hour? Even as he watched, a light wagon appeared, passing a lantern on the west end of town. It too was filled with townsfolk. Preacher's brow burrowed in perplexity. What was this? A mass exodus from Ten Sleep? Three men galloped into view on horseback, following the light wagon.

Preacher didn't know what to think. The folks in Ten Sleep might stampede to the south if they believed an Indian attack was imminent. But except for the Cheyenne war party he'd encountered, and the friendly Nez Perce, Preacher hadn't seen any Indian signs. An Indian attack on

Ten Sleep was unlikely. Then why were so many people leaving?

A man and a woman in a buggy became visible, joining the general evacuation.

Impelled by his curiosity, Preacher rode into Ten Sleep.

A man on a horse rode out of the livery, past the man in black. "If you know what's good for you, stranger," the man called, "you'll skeddaddle!"

Before Preacher could respond, the man was gone.

Ten Sleep was deathly still. The man on the horse must have been the last one to leave. The wind whipped the dusty street.

Preacher wondered if the town was deserted. He spied four horses, cavalry mounts, in front of the saloon.

The quiet was abruptly punctuated by ribald laughter coming from the Tiger Saloon. So someone was still in Ten Sleep. Preacher rode to the front of the saloon and slid to the ground.

Someone in the saloon was boisteriously cursing a blue streak. A woman screamed.

Preacher went through the swinging doors.

Four inebriated troopers and a woman in a green dress were the only occupants of the saloon, if you didn't count the dead man sprawled upon one of the tables. A soldier sporting muttonchops was behind the bar, a bottle of his left hand. Two others stood in front of the bar. All three were leering and cackling at the antics of the fourth trooper. This one, the youngest, was trying to stick his right hand down the front of the woman's dress. None of them noticed the newcomer's arrival.

The woman, an attractive redhead, was resisting the young trooper as best she could. He'd already torn the top of her dress, exposing the top of her bosom.

"Let's have a looksee!" the man behind the bar yelled. "Tear her dress off, Harry!"

Harry succeeded in plunging his right hand down the dress.

The redhead slapped the young trooper across his face.

Harry bristled and raised his right fist to strike her.

"That's enough!"

The command cracked the air like a whip. All eyes turned

toward the doorway. The troopers did a double take. The woman jerked Harry's hand from her dress and stepped back. She turned silently appealing eyes on the man in black.

The man behind the bar recovered first. "Who the hell are you?" he bellowed. "This is a private party! So git! Pronto!"

Preacher looked at the woman. "Would you like to leave, ma'am?"

The relief on her face was all the answer he needed.

"The lady is leaving with me," Preacher announced.

The man with the muttonchops pounded his right fist on top of the bar. "The hell you say! She's staying right where she is! She's going to provide our entertainment!"

"You won't be needing entertainment," Preacher told him.

"Oh? Why not?" Muttonchops demanded arrogantly.

"Because you'll be dead."

The man behind the bar grinned. "There's four of us, mister and only one of you!" He glanced at his companions. "Four of us and one of him! We can take him!"

They tried.

Harry, the youngest, grabbed for the Starr .44 caliber revolver in his holster. The other three troopers went for their guns. All four were handicapped by the alcohol in their systems and the flaps on their holsters. All four died without clearing leather.

Preacher shot the man behind the bar first, planting a bullet between the man's beady eyes and propelling Muttonchops back against the large mirror behind the bar. Bottles clattered to the floor. Preacher cut down the two in front of the bar next, his two swift shots sounding as one. Each was struck in the forehead. Each staggered into the bar and collapsed.

Harry's hand was on his Starr when Preacher's forty-four forty blasted. Harry's right eye was blown apart, and his head exploded outward, raining blood, hair and brains on the floor behind him. He toppled to the floor and trembled for a moment before his body became motionless.

Preacher glanced at the woman in green. "Any more of them?"

"No," she responded. "Just the four of them."

Preacher quickly reloaded the spent rounds in his hip gun, then returned the gun to its holster.

"Who are you?" the woman asked.

"Preacher. J.D. Preacher."

"I've read about you in the papers," the woman acknowledged. She stared at the four bodies. "Now I can believe what I read."

Preacher walked up to the woman. "What went on here?"

The redhead nodded at the corpses. "Deserters. I don't know where they came from. Kept babbling about digging for gold, and how they were wasting their time in the Army. They showed up in Ten Sleep drunk."

"How'd you get involved?"

"They took me right off the street!" the redhead exclaimed.

"Did this man try to help you?" Preacher asked, indicating the body on the table.

"Him? No. He was killed earlier," the woman answered. She studied him for a moment. "You saved my life, Mister Preacher."

"Just Preacher, ma'am," he said.

"And you can stop with the ma'am," the redhead stated. "I'm Brooke Merriweather. You can call me Brooke. I own the general store here."

"I saw a lot of folks leaving Ten Sleep when I rode in," Preacher mentioned. "What was that all about?"

"The good citizens of Ten Sleep were fleeing for their lives," Brooke replied. She glanced at the bodies and the blood. "I need some fresh air. If you'll walk with me to the store, I'll explain everything."

Preacher moved aside for Brooke to precede him, then trailed after her as she departed the Tiger Saloon and started across the windblown street. Except for the four cavalry horses, the street was still empty. He watched her backside as she walked, her steady stride and a hint of the shapely legs under her dress. Her red hair was lashed by the wind.

For her part, Brooke Merriweather was in a quandary. Here was a man she instinctively sensed she could trust, but a nagging uncertainty clouded her mind. Should she tell Preacher about the girl in the storeroom? Was Preacher after the hapless girl, too? What was the famous Widow Maker

# SLAUGHTER AT TEN SLEEP

doing in a sleepy hollow like Ten Sleep? On a personal level, she'd found herself attracted by the man, by his lanky good looks and virile personality. She hadn't been attracted by a man in a good while, and the stimulation of her dormant sensuality was consequently heightened.

Brooke reached the door to her general store and stepped inside. The lantern on the counter was still burning.

"You own this?" Preacher asked as he came inside.

"Yes," Brooke replied.

Preacher nodded appreciatively. "You've done all right by yourself," he commented.

"For a woman?" Brooke rejoined.

Preacher looked her in the eye. "For anyone."

Brooke regretted baiting him. She leaned on the counter and stared at him. "If you don't mind my asking," she ventured, "what are you doing in Ten Sleep?"

"I'm searching for a girl," Preacher said.

Brooke's fingers tightened on the counter. "A girl? What girl?"

"I'd rather not say," Preacher said.

He didn't know if he could rely on this Merriweather woman, and he wasn't about to reveal his hand until after he ascertained if she was connected in any way to the kidnappers. For all he knew, Brooke might be a relative, a sister or cousin, of the kidnappers. If he told her why he was in Ten Sleep, she might run to her kin and spill the beans.

"Suit yourself," Brooke stated, shrugging. "Would you like something to eat or drink? My store is well stocked."

"Not at the moment, thanks," Preacher said. "I do need some answers, though. Are you the only one left in Ten Sleep?"

"I don't know," Brooke said. "Most likely."

"And the others left because of the deserters," Preacher queried.

"Partly," Brooke stated. "You recall the dead man on the table? He was gunned down earlier by one of the Bascombs."

Preacher's eyes narrowed. "Did you say Bascombs?"

"Yeah. The Bascomb family are the worst bunch of vermin you'd ever want to meet! The man on the table was

Colin Rennert, the owner of the Tiger Saloon. He was gunned down by one of the Bascomb boys. The Bascombs lit out when the deserters rode in. I figure the Bascombs mistook the deserters for an army patrol!"

"How many of these Bascombs are there?" Preacher inquired.

"Eight, all tolled," Brooke said. "Let's see. The youngest pair are Rafe and Rufus, two polecats with a yen for squeezing the trigger."

"They won't be squeezing triggers anymore," Preacher said.

"Oh? What makes you say that?" Brooke asked.

"They're dead," Preacher remarked.

"You?" Brooke probbed.

Preacher simply nodded.

"Then you'd best watch yourself," Brooke warned him. "The other Bascombs are even meaner than Rafe and Rufus were. And they're a close-knit clan. You cross one, you cross all of them."

Preacher glanced at the front door. So now he knew the Bascombs were in Ten Sleep. Or had been. If they'd rode out because of the four troopers, it seemed likely the Bascombs wouldn't return to Ten Sleep until morning. He mentally debated the wisdom of waiting for them.

True, the Bascombs weren't his first priority; Elizabeth Demming was. But the girl was nowhere around, and there was no way of telling where the kidnappers had taken her after leaving the cabin.

If he waited in Ten Sleep until sunup, he might be able to confront the Bascombs and get to the bottom of the Uncle Andy business. Then he could light out after the kidnappers. Lone Eagle might be able to track them if their trail from the cabin wasn't cold. The only solid lead he had was the name of the one kidnapper, the one who'd dictated their terms to General Demming. What was his first name? Sherm. That was it. Preacher decided to ask Brooke if she'd never heard of the man.

"Brooke, you must know most of the folks hereabouts," Preacher said.

"I should," Brooke agreed. "This is the only general store for miles. Everybody comes here for their supplies and such."

"Then you might know the man I'm looking for," Preacher stated. "I don't know his whole name. But his first name is Sh—"

She abruptly stopped speaking as a tremendous crash sounded from the rear of the general store. His vest gun leaped into his right hand.

"Good Lord!" Brooke exclaimed, paling.

"Let's take a look," Preacher proposed.

"You needn't bother," Brooke said hastily. "It's probably my cat."

"You can't afford to take chances with the Bascombs about," Preacher said. He moved past her and around the counter.

"There's no need!" Brooke declared, sticking to his heels.

Preacher kept going, through the curtain and along the short hallway to a closed door. "What's this?"

"My storeroom," Brooke responded.

"Is it locked."

"Yes."

"Open it," Preacher directed.

"You're making a lot of fuss over nothing," Brooke assured him. "Really."

"I'm not about to leave until we know for sure," Preacher said. "Open it."

Brooke frowned and crouched next to the small barrel. She extracted the key and held it up. "This will unlock it."

Preacher took the key and used his left hand to twist it in the lock. He crouched and shoved, flinging the door wide, and moved into the storeroom, his forty-four forty leveled.

A shelf of canned goods was in a heap on the floor. Other cans were scattered about.

Brooke stared at the floor, then scanned the darkened storeroom, bewildered. The girl was gone!

"It appears your shelf broke," Preacher commented, replacing his six shooter.

"What could have caused it, I wonder?" Brooke asked absently, disturbed by the girl's departure.

"You might have overloaded it," Preacher said. "Or it could have been the wind."

"The wind?"

Preacher nodded toward the rear window. "Yeah. Maybe the wind blew it down."

Brooke looked up at the window, comprehending at last. The rear window was gone. Completely busted out. The girl must have climbed the shelves on the wall up to the window, and used a can or something else to break the window and crawl to safety. But why? Why would she flee into the night? Hadn't she trusted Brooke? Or had the girl overheard Preacher's voice and fled out of fear.

"Do you want me to cover that window for you?" Preacher asked.

"No," Brooke answered coldly. "I think you've done enough for one night."

# 17

Elizabeth Demming ran from the rear of the general store, darting to the left between the store and another building, fleeing like a frightened deer from a marauding mountain lion. She had grown tired of waiting in the inky storeroom. She'd called out for the woman named Brooke, but no one had answered. In frustration, she'd thumped on the door and drummed on the walls with a can. But Brooke never came. Fatigued, feeling miserable and lonely, Elizabeth had sank to the floor and tried to rest, but her worry and anxiety got the better of her and all she did was toss and turn.

Finally, voices had sounded from the front of the store. Elizabeth had pressed her ear to the door, and she distinctly heard a male voice. Distorted by the distance and the door, she'd assumed the male voice belonged to Boone Bascomb. The Bascombs had returned! They were going to search the general store for her!

Panic overwhelmed her. Elizabeth had clawed up the shelves on the back wall. Clutching a large can, she had smashed the window to shards and crawled outside, tearing her dress in the process. As her feet lifted from the shelf supporting her weight, she felt the shelf give way and heard the racket it made as it struck the floor.

Now, dashing into the street, Elizabeth spied four horses in front of the Tiger Saloon. The owners must be inside the saloon, she reasoned. No one else was in sight. Seeing her opportunity, she dashed to the nearest horse and mounted. She wheeled the animal and galloped to the west end of Ten Sleep.

No shots or shouts announced her escape.

Elizabeth turned to the south and headed out across the prairie. She knew Ten Sleep was northwest of Fort Laramie. If she continued to the south-southeast, she was bound to run into a settlement or town. Hopefully, the people there would be more receptive to her plight than the folks in Ten Sleep had been. Oblivious to the night noises all around her, she rode ever onward. All she could think of was reaching a safe haven. She lost all track of time.

The eastern sky began to brighten. The stars started to fade. A pink tinge suffused the eastern horizon. Then a crimson blue. Golden rays arched skyward. Birds began singing and chirping. The sun appeared, heralding a new day.

Elizabeth had eaten little during her confinement in the storeroom. She'd found a knife and a can of peaches and consumed half the can. The sweet syrup, though, had bothered her stomach, and so she'd stopped. Now, as her body was jostled by the horse's movements, she wished she'd eaten more food.

The prolonged strain was taking its toll. Weariness pervaded her. She wanted to close her eyes and sleep. The further she went, the harder it became to contentrate. She became fearful of committing an error, of causing the horse to stumble and fall. If her mount broke its leg, she would be stranded in the middle of the prairie with scant chance of a rescue.

Fatigue won out.

Elizabeth reached the top of a narrow gully. Brush grew all along its bottom. The perfect hiding place. She angled the animal to the bottom of the gully. On the gully floor, she was at least ten feet below the outlying plain. No one would know she was there unless they stumbled upon her. She climbed from the horse and tethered it to a small bush near a patch of grass.

The horse craned its neck to nibble on the grass.

Elizabeth suddenly recognized the animal as a cavalry mount. What had it been doing in Ten Sleep? There had been three others, hadn't there? That meant a cavalry patrol! Some of her father's men out hunting for her! And she'd stupidly fled Ten Sleep!

Elizabeth hesitated. Should she catch some sleep or return to Ten Sleep? If she slept, she risked the cavalrymen being gone when she got back. She wanted to ride back, but she knew she was too tired to be trusted in the saddle. An hour or two wouldn't make a difference. The townspeople were bound to tell the soldiers about the Bascombs. The soldiers, in turn, would contact her father. Her rescue was assured!

The horse was eating some of the grass.

Elizabeth sighed as she lowered herself to the ground under a stunted tree. She laid on her back, bone weary, and placed her hands under her neck. An hour or two, she told herself, that was all she needed. An hour or two. She closed her eyes, then opened them again.

Something was wrong.

The sun, just above the eastern horizon when she'd laid down, was now directly overhead. The heat on her face had awakened her.

Elizabeth sat up. She'd overslept! She must have dozed for six or seven hours! She had to leave for Ten Sleep immediately. She rose and turned, thinking the worst of her ordeal was behind her. But she was wrong.

The horse was gone.

Dumbfounded, Elizabeth looked to the right and the left. She shuffled forward, dazed. Where could it have gone, she wondered? Now she was afoot without food and water in hostile territory. No! She climbed to the top of the gully and looked for her mount on the vastness of the prairie.

Nothing.

Elizabeth began walking to the north. She knew Ten Sleep was in that general direction. But she had no idea what might lie to the south, west, or east. There might be a settlement to the south, but how far? She wouldn't be able to travel any great distance on foot. Ten Sleep was her best bet.

The afternoon sun baked the earth. Little life stirred. A bird or two winged through the sky. A jack rabbit hopped into the distance.

Elizabeth struggled onward. Sweat trickled down her arms and legs. After several hours, her lips became slightly puffy and dry. The June sun elevated the temperatures into the eighties.

Several pronghorn appeared far to the east. They idly watched her passage, perhaps attracted by her white dress, now dirty and torn.

Elizabeth tried to disregard the heat and the lack of water. If she stopped, she was dead. She tried to recall some of the stories her father had told her about the plainsmen, about how the scouts survived, about the tricks of their trade, the knowledge they used to acquire water. Wasn't there a plant of some sort alleged to contain all the water a human would need? She couldn't recollect its name or appearance.

A turkey vulture soared overhead. It wheeled on the wind, hovering over the figure in white below.

Elizabeth squinted up at the vulture. She knew it was sizing her up, assessing her ability to endure. If the vulture sensed she was weak, was faltering, it would stay with her, waiting for her to drop and die. A meal on the hoof, so to speak.

"Go away!" Elizabeth shouted upward.

The vulture was unimpressed by her vocal display. It sailed serenely on the wind, watching her.

"Go away, you rotten buzzard!" Elizabeth screamed.

The buzzard took her verbal abuse in stride. Too add insult to injury, it was joined by another. And another.

"Gather the whole family, why don't you?" Elizabeth muttered.

She resolved to deny the buzzards the satisfaction of feasting on her carcass. Her legs surged forward. Ever northward. Ever northward.

The buzzards glided on the air ever with her.

Elizabeth gradually lost her strength and energy. Her legs plodded in a weaving line. Her nap had failed to reviltalize her. She desperately needed food and water. Especially water. Her fancy dress felt like it weighed a ton.

Four more buzzards added themselves to the aerial convention.

Elizabeth peered at the sun. It was now high in the sky, on its downward slant toward the western horizon. Her right foot caught in a rut and she stumbled and tripped, falling to one knee. She pressed her palms against the compact soil and heaved erect.

Two more buzzards linked up with the feathered congregation overhead.

How many were there now? Elizabeth tried to count them but they wouldn't stay still, constantly circling, sailing this way and that. She shuffled ahead, and started to giggle. After she returned to Fort Laramie, she promised herself, she would take her father's rifle and ride out, perhaps with one of the handsome junior officers as an escort. She would ride miles from the fort and she would spend a delightful afternoon shooting every lousy buzzard she saw! What a marvelous idea! She snickered, pleased by her brilliance.

Teach them buzzards a thing or two!

Elizabeth stopped, her mind spinning. Dizziness engulfed her, and she sagged to her knees. What was happening? Why wouldn't her legs do as she told them? She must rise and walk to Ten Sleep! She must!

Oddly, thunder rent the blue sky above her. At least, she thought it was thunder. And there was a great swirling motion, and dust was flying into her face, into her mouth and nose. She tried to breathe, but her lungs seemed to have stepped out for tea.

Elizabeth Cole Demming gasped once, then fell forward onto her face.

# 18

Late afternoon, and the Bascombs still hadn't put in an appearance.

Preacher, standing in the doorway to the Tiger Saloon, frowned. He'd miscalculated. The Bascombs must have left the territory. They evidently weren't returning to Ten Sleep today. And if he couldn't settle his personal business, then finding the Demming girl became his major concern. He'd spent the day in the saloon, waiting.

Brooke Merriweather had done a peculiar about-face. After acting so friendly at first, she'd changed to ice and politely, but forcefully, asked him to leave her store. So he'd walked over to the saloon. After dragging the five bodies out back, he'd settled in to await the Bascombs.

But no Bascombs.

Preacher walked outside. Strips of jerky and Teton Jack taken from behind the bar had been his noon meal. He'd decided to ride out to the cabin, see if the kidnappers were there. Once he'd disposed of those bastards, he could return to Ten Sleep and see if the Bascombs were back. He started to mount his horse.

"Preacher! Wait!"

Preacher glanced at the general store.

Brooke Merriweather, resplendent in a red dress, was hurrying toward him. Smiling, no less.

Who could figure women?

"Preacher, I'm sorry for the way I behaved last night," Brooke told him. "I'd like to make it up to you. After all, you did save my life."

"What did you have in mind?" Preacher asked her.

"My living quarters are above the store," Brooke said. "I was hoping you might join me for supper."

Preacher considered her proposal.

"The Bascombs might come back," Brooke added by way of incentive. "You wouldn't want to miss them, would you?"

"No," Preacher admitted.

"And didn't you say something about hunting someone else?" Brooke reminded him. "We could discuss it over our meal. Like I said before, I know most of the folks hereabouts."

Preacher liked the notion. "You might save me some time at that. I'll come."

"Excellent!"

Brooke turned, making for the store. She'd been thinking about Preacher all day, wondering if she'd jumped the gun. Perhaps Preacher wasn't the reason the girl had fled. He had gunned down the troopers to save her, hadn't he? He couldn't be all bad. And to top it off, Brooke couldn't forget his handsome features. She'd daydreamed about his strong hands on her body.

Preacher followed Brooke into her store. He watched her lock the front door and display her CLOSED FOR BUSINESS sign.

"Won't your customers get a mite riled?" he inquired.

"What customers?" Brooke replied. "We're the only two people in Ten Sleep."

"Those folks who left last night will be back," Preacher said.

"Those yellow bellies?" Brooke retorted. "Not for days."

Preacher accompanied her to the northwest corner of the room. A recessed door was obscured by one of the tall shelves.

"You should be flattered," Brooke told him over her left shoulder. "There isn't an unmarried man in Ten Sleep who hasn't wanted to walk up these stairs at one time or another."

A short flight of steps led up to her living quarters.

Preacher ascended the stairs and discovered a comfortably furnished apartment with an area for cooking, a parlor, and a bedroom.

"Take a seat," Brooke said, nodding toward a plush chair in the parlor.

Preacher moved the chair up to the window fronting the street, then sank into the quilted cushions. "This is a nice place you have here," he complimented her.

"I like it," Brooke stated. She was busy at the wood burning stove. Pots clanged. Pans rattled.

Preacher surveyed the street in both directions. His stallion and the three cavalry mounts were still in front of the saloon directly across the way. He'd fed and watered all four animals earlier. There was no call for the cavalry animals to suffer just because their owners had gotten themselves killed.

"Do you like to eat beef steak?" Brooke called out.

"It's the second favorite thing I like to eat," Preacher answered her.

Brooke walked over to the chair, her eyes sparkling, wiping her hands on a blue towel. She licked her red lips. "Second favorite? What's your first?"

Preacher slowly stood. His eyes locked on her. "Guess," he said softly.

Brooke stared at his face, his chest, then lower. She dropped the towel onto the floor. "The food can always wait," she commented huskily.

Preacher took her into his arms. He pressed his lips against hers, and her mouth parted to receive his tongue. Their kiss lingered and lingered.

Brooke uttered a tiny moan.

Preacher lowered his mouth to her neck.

"You don't waste time, do you?" Brooke asked, her voice a throaty purr.

Preacher didn't bother to respond. He let his lips do his talking. His hands roved over her full figure, over her bosom and buttocks. He began undressing her, wanting to feel her naked flesh touching his skin. In short order, her red dress was on the floor at their feet. Then her undergarments.

Brooke removed his frock coat and unbuttoned his white shirt.

Preacher lifted her into his arms and moved into the bedroom. A large canopy bed filled the room. He deposited her on top of the bedcover, then finished undressing. He slipped the forty-four forties under the white down pillow.

Brooke lifted her right hand and beckoned for him to join her.

Preacher embraced her, their bodies flush, skin against tingling skin, their tongues touching. His firm hands pinched her erect nipples and squeezed her big breasts.

Brooke groaned.

Preacher licked a path from her mouth to her breasts, dawdled on her nipples, then descended to her pubic mound. He ran his fingers through her pubic hair. His mouth sank between her legs, and she arched her back when he suddenly licked her opening.

"Ahhh! Preacher!"

Preacher stuck his tongue into her and swirled it around, savoring her tangy taste.

Brooke began running her hands over her breasts.

Preacher licked and lapped, her inner thighs growing wetter and wetter. He nuzzled into her.

"Yes!" Brooke cried.

Preacher kept at it until her body was quivering. She trembled at his slightest touch. He rose to his hands and knees and aligned his member, then abruptly plunged into her moist box.

"Ahhhhh!" Brooke buried her nails in his back.

Preacher took her right nipple into his mouth and flicked it with his tongue. His hand squeezed her other breast.

"Mmmmmmm," Brooke moaned.

Preacher locked his lips on hers.

Brooke ground her hips into him, swaying her thighs, feeling the heated friction inside of her caused by his engorged organ. He began stroking her, moving in and almost out, in and almost out, sending throbbing pulsations rippling through her body.

Preacher deliberately paced himself. He didn't want to rush. She responded superbly to his every move. He wanted her to enjoy this as much as he was, and he did his utmost to please her.

Brooke raked her nails across his back, then reached up and grabbed his thick hair, tugging on it. She shifted her mouth to his left ear and nibbled on the lobe.

Preacher felt her hot, moist breath prickle his ear. He reached underneath and placed is hands, palms up, under her fanny, and lifted, angling her bottom for maximum effect. Then he rammed into her.

Brooke grunted in surprise. "Oh! Yes! More!"

Preacher gave her more, increasing his pace and slamming himself into her again and again and again. His stroking attained a feverish pitch.

"Ahhhh! Don't stop, Preacher! MORE!"

Preacher pounded into her with a vengeance. Their glistening bodies, caked with sweat, slapped together.

"I'm coming!" Brooke cried, enraptured. "Coming! Ahhhhhhh!"

Preacher came too, trembling, burying his organ inside of her, his body pulsing. An exquisite sensation enveloped his entire form. They thrashed and pumped and gasped and sighed.

And, for a moment at least, their world was at peace.

# 19

"This don't figure!" Ira Bascomb snapped. "Where the hell is Cy?"

"And why are the blue bellies still lookin' for the gold," Sherm asked. "I thought they were after us!"

The Bascombs were on the south rim of Ten Sleep Canyon. Far below them and to the east, General Demming's troopers were actively searching for the hidden gold.

Hidden by a low outcropping, Ira raised on his toes and peeked down at the damn Yankees. "This don't make no sense!" he declared. "When Boone saw that Yankee patrol ridin' into Ten Sleep, I was sure they were comin' after us. That's why we lit out. But maybe they wasn't! Maybe they was just comin' in for supplies."

"That still don't tell us why Cy ain't here," Port commented.

"Think the blue bellies got him?" Burt asked.

"Cy would never get himself caught by Yankees," Boone stated. "Somethin' else must have caused him to leave."

"But where did he go?" Ira demanded angrily. "Cy told you he'd stick with the Yankees until one of us spelled him. He knows how important keepin' an eye on the blue bellies is to our plan!"

"Maybe somethin' happened," Sherm speculated.

"Maybe the Yankees found some of the gold and he rode to tell us."

Ira pointed into the canyon. "Does it look like the blue bellies have found the gold? Look at 'em! They're like little blue ants! They haven't found those gold bars. If they had found some, they would've found the rest by now."

"All this palaver is gettin' us nowhere," Boone said. "All we're doin' is makin' wild guesses. We know Cy ain't here. The question is; where did he go? To Ten Sleep? No. We'd have seen him. Or passed him on our way here. To the cabin? He might have gone there. He didn't know we were in Ten Sleep, and he might have swung around the town. He doesn't know the girl got away from us. The cabin gets my vote."

"What do we do, Pa?" Burt inquired.

Ira shook his bearded head, annoyed. "I had this all planned out! I told each of you what to do way in advance! Now it's all unravelin'! If we don't fetch that girl back, we can forget all 'bout the gold!"

"But what do we do, Pa?" Burt persisted. "What about brother Cy?"

"We'll go find your brother," Ira said, mounting up. "We'll ride to the cabin first. If he ain't there, we'll ride into Ten Sleep after dark."

"What if he ain't at either place?" Burt asked.

"He'd better be," Ira stated sternly.

Boone nodded toward Ten Sleep Canyon. "What about the blue bellies, Pa? Shouldn't one of us stay put and keep watch?"

"Forget 'em for now," Ira said. "They won't go nowheres. Besides, if we don't get that girl, it won't matter one way or the other if the Yankees find the gold." He swept his right arm forward. "Let's burn the breeze!"

# 20

Had she died and gone to Heaven? Or the other place?

Elizabeth could hear voices nearby. She strained, endeavoring to catch their drift. But the individual words were too indistinct. Graduually, her sluggish senses identified some of the words. "... might.... is.... around." Was it an angel, she wondered? She wanted to touch the speaker, to see for sure. Fingers took hold of hers and held on tight.

".... is comin' around!" a male voice declared excitedly.

Were angels men or women? She couldn't recall. Elizabeth opened her eyes.

A handsome cavalry officer was bent over her, peering intently into her face. "She's awake!" he shouted. "Bring the canteen!"

Elizabeth was lying on an army blanket. She tried to speak, but her swollen lips refused to cooperate and form the words.

"You rest easy, Miss Demming," the officer said. "I'm Lieutenant James. That there is Lone Eagle," he stated, pointing to the right.

An elderly Indian was walking toward them bearing a canteen.

"You're lucky to be alive," Lieutenant James said. "We figured you for a goner when we spotted you!"

Lone Eagle reached their side and offered the canteen to the officer.

Lieutenant James hastily uncapped the canteen.

"Not too much," Lone Eagle cautioned. "Sip."

Lieutenant James eased his left hand under Elizabeth's head and tilted her upwards. "Here. Just a sip! You drink too much, and you'll be sick."

Elizabeth felt cool water dribble on her puffy lips and chin. Some of the liquid seeped into her mouth, and her greedy tongue swirled it around. She swallowed, and never, ever, had water tasted so good.!

"I've been lookin' all over creation for you," Lieutenant James told her as he allowed more water to enter her mouth. "I just about gave up hope! We were on our way into Ten Sleep when Lone Eagle saw all these buzzards circlin' way south of us." He paused. "Lone Eagle has got eyes like a hawk."

"Or eagle," Lone Eagle amended, grinning.

"If it hadn't of been for the buzzards," Lieutenant James elaborated, "we'd of never found you."

So! The rotten buzzards had done some good, after all! Elizabeth wanted to laugh, but couldn't.

"You rest," Lieutenant James advised her. "We'll wait 'till the sun sets. Then we should see about gettin' you to Ten Sleep. There might be someone there who can help. You have some nasty blisters on your feet. I imagine it was awful hard walkin' in those fine shoes of yours."

Elizabeth stared into the officer's eyes. If she could have mustered the strength, she would have hugged him and given him a big kiss in gratitude for her rescue.

"Wait'll your father sees you!" Lieutenant James remarked. "Won't he be surprised! Maybe he'll decide to go easy on me."

Elizabeth was puzzled by his last comment.

"I even found you before Preacher," Lieutenant James bragged.

He glanced down at Elizabeth. "Did you know your father hired the Widow Maker? J.D. Preacher is his name. One of the best gunhands there is. There's few better. Hickok, maybe, could take him. We were with Preacher last night, but he snuck off on us. I suspect he might be in Ten Sleep." He paused. "Well, if he is, he doesn't get to take you back. I

# SLAUGHTER AT TEN SLEEP

found you, and I'll take you to your father!" he promised her.

Elizabeth, feeling drowsy, closed her eyes. His ceaseless prattle soothed her, comforted her. It was reassuring to have someone's arms around her after her harrowing ordeal.

"I need to ask a few questions," Lieutenant James said. "Don't bother tryin' to speak. Simply nod yes or shake your head no. Do you understand?"

Elizabeth slowly nodded.

"Are the kidnappers hereabouts?" James asked.

Elizabeth shook her head.

"Do you know where they might be?"

Eliabeth nodded, opening her eyes.

"Where? We were at their cabin last night, and they never showed up. Where did you see 'em last? Out here somewhere?"

Elizabeth signified in the negative.

"At their cabin?" James queried her.

Again, she shook her head.

"In Ten Sleep?"

Elizabeth nodded vigorously.

"Ten Sleep, huh?" Lieutenant James scratched his chin. "Then we'd best be careful when we ride into town. I wish there was somewhere closer we could take you, but Ten Sleep is the nearest settlement. Don't worry, though, Lone Eagle and I will protect you."

Lone Eagle, squatting a few yards away, glanced at the lieutenant. "But who protects Lone Eagle and Little Britches?"

Lieutenant James ignored the scout. "I don't know if you recollect it," he said to Elizabeth, "but we have met before. We've greeted each other a few times at Fort Laramie. Do you remember?" he inquired hopefully.

Elizabeth was about to shake her head, but she paused, noting the expectant expression on his face. For the first time, she noticed the look in his eyes when he stared at her. He was interested in her! She mustered a feeble grin and nodded.

Lieutenant James puffed up. "I knew you would! After you've recovered, and if you're willin', I'd like to see a lot more of you. You think about it, all right?"

Elizabeth nodded. She closed her eyes and drifted off.

Lieutenant James glanced at Lone Eagle and winked, grinning from ear to ear.

Lone Eagle gazed to the west, observing a dark cloud bank on the far horizon. A storm was brewing. He hoped it wouldn't strike before they reached Ten Sleep, or some other shelter. Storms could be especially fierce on the Wyoming Territory prairie. He glanced at Little Britches and the general's daughter, hoping the approaching storm wasn't an omen, a warning from the spirits.

# 21

"Anyone for a third helping?"

Preacher looked at the redhead beside him. She'd been one of the most stimulating bed partners he'd ever shared a kiss with, and he was reluctant to climb from under the sheets. But he could see the front window from where he rested, and the sky was growing dark.

"I'd like to, Brooke. I truly would. Maybe later." He eased from the bed and began dressing.

"Any time, big man," Brooke said. She raised on her right elbow and watched him don his shirt. "Why the rush?"

"I've dallied long enough. Too long," Preacher said. He studied her face, her green eyes, deciding whether he could rely on her. He could. "I've got to cut the trail of the kidnappers."

Brooke's brow furrowed. "Kidnappers?"

"Is there a telegraph in Ten Sleep?" Preacher asked as he slipped his left foot into a boot.

"No."

"Then I reckon you haven't heard the news," Preacher said. "The daughter of General Nels Demming was kidnapped from Fort Laramie?"

"Kidnapped?" Brooke sat up. "Why would anyone kidnap her?"

"Two reasons that I can see," Preacher stated, putting on

his right boot. "The first is money. Gold bars. The gold the army stashed away in Ten Sleep Canyon."

"But that gold's been lost for years," Brooke mentioned. "No one knows where it is," she paused, "if it really exists."

"It exists," Preacher assured her. "And that brings us to the second reason Demming's daughter was abducted. The kidnappers needed a lot of men to do the searching for them. They're using her as a hostage to spur the general and his men into finding the gold. I aim to track them down and return the girl to her father."

"She's the girl you mentioned before?"

"Yes," Preacher answered.

Brooke thought of the girl in the storeroom. Her hands clutched the sheet until her knuckles were white. "What does this girl look like?"

"I haven't seen her," Preacher stated, "but General Demming gave me a description. Long black hair, a white dress—"

"Dear Lord!" Brooke exclaimed.

Preacher was startled by the horrified expression contorting her face. "What is it?"

"She was here!" Brooke blurted.

"Demming's daughter? Elizabeth?" Preacher knelt on the bed.

Brooke nodded. "I didn't know her name! I didn't know she'd been kidnapped! She wanted a place to hide, so I put her in the storeroom!"

"The storeroom? But I saw your storeroom, remember? There was no one . . ." Preacher said, and stopped. "The window!" he exclaimed. "It wasn't the wind! It was the girl!"

"That's my guess," Brooke agreed.

Preacher resisted an impulse to smash his fist into the wall. He'd been so close! But why had the girl fled? Had she heard his voice and mistaken him for one of the kidnappers?

"I should never have let myself be sidetracked by the Bascombs," he said regretfully.

The Bascombs! Brooke sat forward. Elizabeth Demming had been running from the Bascombs! Could it be? "Do you know the identity of the kidnappers?"

Preacher frowned. "No. I wish to blazes I did. All I have to go on are a couple of first names. One of them, a hardcase called Cy, is dead. The other one is a gunny named Sherm—"

Brooke's right hand darted out, covering Preacher's mouth. Her features were a study in astonishment. "Preacher! You've been after the kidnappers all along!" She removed her hand.

"What?" Preacher asked in consternation.

"Yes!" Brooke declared. "The girl I hid in my storeroom was trying to escape from the *Bascombs*! Colin Rennert was gunned down by Sherm *Bascomb*! Cy was another of the *Bascombs*! You said last night you were looking for the Bascombs because of Rafe and Rufus. Well, apparently you've been hunting for the kidnappers and didn't even know it!"

Preacher slowly stood. A great and terrible transformation was taking place. His facial lines tightened, his mouth becoming a thin slit. His eyes narrowed with furious intensity.

"Preacher?" Brooke said.

Preacher's head turned in her direction. Brooke inadvertently recoiled. Only minutes before, this man she'd loved had been in repose, his face relaxed, at ease. Now his expression was enough to freeze a rabid dog in its tracks. She imagined she could see his eyes smoldering. If Death had a face, then she knew she was looking at it.

"Preacher?" she said weakly.

Preacher walked to the doorway.

"Preacher? Are you coming back?" Brooke called.

Preacher didn't answer. He left her apartment, stepped down the stairs, and crossed to the front door. His mind was a seething cauldron of self recrimination. It was his sister, Abigail, all over again! A woman desperately needing his help, and he was failing to deliver! He opened the door and stepped into the street.

Dusk was blanketing Ten Sleep in a musty twilight.

A pounding of hoofs sounded to the east, and six members of the U.S. Army rode into view, coming down the middle of the street, led by a captain. He raised his right hand and called for a halt, and the patrol came to a stop between Preacher and the three cavalry mounts hitched in front of the Tiger Saloon.

The captain glanced at the military mounts, then at the man in black. "You!" he barked. "Do you know where the men owning these mounts are? I was sent out by General Nels Demming to find five deserters. Those horses belong to three of the men who deserted their posts. I'm looking for a Lieutenant James and four privates."

Preacher started around the captain's horse.

"I'm talking to you, mister!" the captain snapped. "Do you know where I can find these men?"

Preacher halted, his arms at his side. He stared up at the captain. "You'll find the four privates behind the saloon. Dead."

"Dead?" the captain reiterated. "Who killed them?"

"I did," Preacher said, and resumed walking.

"Hold on!" the captain shouted, moving his horse in front of the man in black, blocking his path. The captain's right hand rested on his holster flap. "You killed them? Why?"

"Ask them," Preacher said, starting around the captain's horse once more.

"Stop!" the captain ordered. He waved his left arm, and his men fanned out across the street. Two of them held their carbines. "I'm warning you!"

Preacher spun. His eyes bored into the captain. "Don't tell me what to do!"

"You're under arrest," the captain stated.

"For what?"

"For the murder of four soldiers," the captain said.

"They were deserters!" Preacher rejoined. "And they pulled on me!"

"That doesn't concern me," the captain declared angrily. "You can justify your actions at your trial. Now hand over your hardware!"

Preacher was on the edge. The years of fighting the Union troops, the countless battles and bloodletting, the destruction of his native land caused by the plundering Yankees and the vile carpetbaggers, all paraded before his mind's eye.

"Hand it over!" the bellicose captain insisted, "or I'll order my men to fire!"

The troopers with the carbines lowered their barrels in Preacher's direction.

"Don't do something you'll regret," Preacher stated

# SLAUGHTER AT TEN SLEEP

coldly.

"This is your last warning!" the captain yelled.

"You'd best talk to General Demming," Preacher suggested.

"Quit stalling! I want your hardware now!"

"Go to hell."

Instead, the irate captain foolishly went for his revolver.

Preacher, his emotional control strained to its limit and beyond, crouched and drew, his hip gun up and out in a twinkling. The first booming shot from the forty-four forty blew out the captain's forehead and sent the officer flying from his horse.

Despite being outnumbered and exposed, with no cover within ten feet, Preacher actually had an edge over the five remaining troopers. They weren't professional gunmen. The army didn't require ordinary soldiers to be exceptional marksmen. In addition, the holsters the troopers wore were all the flapped variety, covered by a leather flap to keep the gun in place and keep out the dust. The troopers had to move the flap aside, and then reach into their holster to grab their sidearm. This took precious seconds, seconds they could ill afford to waste when their lives were on the line.

But two of the troopers already had their carbines unlimbered; they didn't need to slap leather. One of them holding a carbine fired, the slug stirring the dust between Preacher's legs.

Preacher's next shot ripped out that trooper's left eye and tore through his brain. The trooper landed in the street on his back.

Four to go.

Preacher swiveled, going for the second soldier with a carbine in his hands, but the soldier's horse reared as he fired, and his shot missed the soldier's head by a fraction.

The soldier shot at the man in black, and the bullet tugged on Preacher's right sleeve as it nicked his coat.

Preacher aimed a second shot at the soldier, but even as he squeezed the trigger, the soldier, in the act of striving to control his rearing mount, his arm holding the carbine waving wildly, wagged the carbine in the air, its barrel inches from his head. The action saved his life. Temporarily. The slug from Preacher's forty-four forty smashed into the carbine barrel and was deflected into the ground. The carbine was nearly wrenched from the soldier's hand, but he retained his grip as his horse came down on all fours, its hoofs flailing and slashing at the man in black.

Preacher ducked under those raking hoofs to the right, and he fired as the soldier twisted toward him. He fired again as the soldier tried to club him with the carbine barrel. The soldier toppled from the saddle.

The hip gun was empty!

The remaining three soldiers were still game, two clawing for their sidearms while the third frantically attempted to pull his carbine from its scabbard.

One of the troopers cleared leather and fired, his shot missing Preacher's right ear by a hair's breadth.

Preacher was moving to the right, toward the saloon.

The trooper steadied his gun hand, wanting to be sure this time.

Neighing in a fright caused by all the gunfire, the captain's mount bolted, plunging between the three soldiers and the man in black. For an instant, Preacher was blotted from view, and in that instant he turned the tide.

Preacher employed a tactic he'd rarely used in a shooting scrape, but had practiced on many an occasion. He border shifted, transferring the hip gun to his left hand with a deft flip, even as his right hand streaked to his vest gun, so that when the captain's mount was past him and racing to the west, Preacher was ready. He cut loose, three incredibly swift shots, all head aimed, and the three soldiers joined their companions in death, their bodies convulsing and shuddering as they expired.

Several other of their mounts bolted, following the first.

Preacher, his face an iron mask, slowly straightened.

One of the troopers was moaning piteously.

Preacher proceeded to eject the spent cartridges and insert new ones into the chambers of his weapons.

Another of the troopers began gurgling and wheezing.

Preacher, his weapons reloaded, walked up to the prone soldiers. Four were dead, but two of them still lived, both with mortal wounds. Both might linger for hours in acute agony, but neither could be saved.

There was only one course to take.

Preacher shot the first trooper in the head, waited for the

soldier to stop twitching, then walked to the second one and performed a similar act of mercy.

The street in Ten Sleep was suddenly quiet.

Preacher immediately replaced the pair of spent cartridges. As he gazed as his fallen foes, he recollected the last time he had downed six men in a single fight. It had been shortly after the War. He'd been on his way home, to Bradburn Hill plantation, and he had stopped at Glen-Elyn Horse Farms to rest. Seven carpetbaggers had tried to plunder Glen-Elyn; he'd killed six of them in a brutal fight.

A gusty breeze from the west causéd a swirl of fine dust to settle on the corpses.

Preacher, his weapons reloaded and in their holsters, walked over to his horse and climbed aboard. He stared at the dead troopers for a moment, realizing the army would be on his heels once the story about the Ten Sleep gunfight spread. Then again, with Ten Sleep deserted, who would inform them?

He began to wheel to the west, and his gaze fell on the apartment window above the general store. Brooke Merriweather, clad in a green robe, was standing at her window, her mouth slack, gawking at the carnage he'd wrought.

Preacher grimly nodded at her, then rode into the night and the gathering storm.

## 22

"How much further do we have to go?" Lieutenant James asked.

"Some miles yet," Lone Eagle replied.

"How many?" Lieutenant James wanted specifics.

"Some," Lone Eagle responded.

They were riding toward Ten Sleep. The westerly wind was increasing in force by the hour, and gray clouds were swirling overhead. Flashing bolts of lightning occasionally appeared in the western sky and infrequently they heard the faint rumble of thunder. The sun had set almost an hour ago.

Lone Eagle was in the lead.

Lieutenant James, five yards behind the Crow scout, could feel Elizabeth Demming's arms encircling his waist. They were both on his mount, and she was leaning against his back for support.

"How are you holdin' up, Elizabeth?"

"Fine," Elizabeth mumbled. Her lips functioned again, but forming words was difficult.

"You hold on tight," Lieutenant James encouraged her. "We'll be in Ten Sleep before you know it."

"What if the Bascombs are there? The kidnappers, I mean?" she asked.

"Bascombs? Is that the name of the men responsible for

## SLAUGHTER AT TEN SLEEP

takin' you from Fort Laramie?"

"Yes," Elizabeth answered. "Badmen through and through. I pray we don't run into them."

"Don't fret," Lieutenant James said. "Lone Eagle and I will defend you to the death."

Lone Eagle glanced back, but didn't say a word.

"There are six of them," Elizabeth detailed. "You must watch out for them! Their Pa, as they like to call him, is their leader. His name is Ira. The rest are his sons. Sherm is the pistoleer. Boone is sort of a mountain man. Cy and Port are unsavory types. And Burt, he's the youngest. Please don't let them catch me again!"

"They won't," James assured her. He pondered for a few minutes. "Tell you what I'll do. When we reach Ten Sleep, Lone Eagle will ride in ahead of us and look the town over. If he spots trouble, we'll keep goin' to Ten Sleep Canyon. If he doesn't see any sign of these Bascombs, we'll spend the rest of the night in Ten Sleep and ride to the canyon tomorrow. How does that idea sound?"

"Sounds fine," Elizabeth said. "I can't wait to see my father again. I thought he'd given up on me."

"Genral Demming never gave up on you," Lieutenant James informed her. "He has one hundred men scourin' Ten Sleep Canyon for the lost gold. And, like I mentioned before, he hired the Widow Maker to find you. Your father has been doin' all he can. Don't be too hard on him."

"I won't be," Elizabeth said.

The trio rode onward. The wind continued to whip them. The clouds were darkening.

"We hurry!" Lone Eagle called back. "Storm be here quick!"

"Let's go, then!" Lieutenant James yelled.

They picked up the gait. The lightning flashes were closer now. The thunder was louder.

Elizabeth pressed her right cheek against Lieutenant James' coat and closed her eyes. The motion of his horse had caused a queasy sensation to develop in her stomach. She desperately craved a hot meal and a hotter bath. Her father's image popped into her mind. How could she have doubted him, she asked herself? Her father would make the Bascombs pay for the indignities she had suffered! The Bascombs would rue the day they were born!

The lashing wind momentarily stopped.

Elizabeth was struck by a thought. "Why me?" she asked.

"Beg pardon?" Lieutenant James responded.

"Why me? Why did the Bascombs take me?" Elizabeth questioned him.

"If my memory serves," Lieutenant James said, "only one other fort commander in the Wyoming Territory has a daughter, and she's livin' back east. The others have sons. These Bascombs probably figured it'd be easier abductin' a daughter than a son."

"You think that's all there was to it?" Elizabeth queried.

"It's just a hunch on my part," Lieutenant James remarked. "But I wouldn't think it's far off the mark."

The rest of their ride was conducted in silence as Lone Eagle led them at a faster pace, and Lieutenant James concentrated on keeping up.

The wind from the west gained strength, redoubled its speed.

Lieutenant James hardly paid attention to the building storm. He was happier than he'd been in months. He'd saved the woman of his dreams, and his prospects for courting her were greatly heightened in the bargain. There was the little matter of abandoning his post at Ten Sleep Canyon, but he fervently hoped the general would forgive him. Surely General Demming could overlook a minor indiscretion when all the factors were considered? Surely the general would be so elated at having his daughter returned safely, he would pardon the man responsible for snatching her from the jaws of death?

"Ten Sleep!" Lone Eagle unexpectedly shouted.

Lieutenant James spurred his mount and caught up with the Crow. "Where?"

Lone Eagle pointed.

By squinting, Lieutenant James was able to distinguish the tall outline of clustered structures ahead. But there was no evidence of any lanterns. Perhaps the wind had blown them out. "Ride in and take note of who is there. Then report back."

Lone Eagle hesitated. He frowned and urged his horse toward Ten Sleep.

A few light drops of rain spattered the ground.

Lone Eagle hefted his Winchester as he rode into the west

end off Ten Sleep. Every lantern in town appeared to be out. He knew the wind might be responsible for extinguishing some, but the rest either had never been lit or had burned all their fuel. He paused, surveying the street. Where were all the people?

A light suddenly appeared inside of the Tiger Saloon. A faint glow illuminated the street in front of the saloon.

Lone Eagle's eyes widened.

Six bodies were lying in the street. All wore uniforms. All in attitudes of violent death. Otherwise, the street was deserted. Not even a horse present.

Lone Eagle rode up to the saloon and dropped to the earth. He cautiously walked to the swinging doors and peered inside.

A lovely white woman, a redhead in a green dress, was seated at a table near the bar. A lantern was in front of her, and a smoking match was to her left. Between the woman and the lantern was a half-empty whiskey bottle.

Lone Eagle entered the saloon.

The redhead turned and spotted him. She laughed and raised the bottle to her lips, then smirked at him. "Kill me and get it over with!" she cried, her words slightly slurred, spreading her arms wide.

Lone Eagle moved over to her table. "What happened here?"

"Happened?" the redhead responded, snickering. "I'll tell you what's *happening*! I'm doing something I haven't done in ages! Ages! I'm drinking myself under the table. Would you like to join me?"

Lone Eagle shook his head. "Where townspeople?"

"Gone!" the rehead replied. "All gone! Even the horses! I sent them on their way."

"Dead bluecoats in street," Lone Eagle commented.

The redhead raised her right hand, her first finger extended and her thumb cocked like a revolver hammer. "Cut them down!" she said, giggling. "All of them! Never saw the like in all my born days!" She made loud popping sounds, as if she was firing a gun.

Lone Eagle was confused. Dead soldiers all over the place. A crazy white woman drinking herself into a stupor. And no one else in town. Even for white people, this was loco. "You stay here," he told the woman.

The redhead laughed. "Honey, old Brooke ain't going anywhere! Go get the scalping party! We'll have a ball!" She giggled and giggled.

Lone Eagle hurried outside and mounted. He rode from Ten Sleep, the wind buffeting his body, the rain pelting his face.

"What did you find?" Lieutenant James demanded as the scout rode up.

"Must see yourself," Lone Eagle said.

"Why? What did you find?" Lieutenant James questioned him.

"Come. See." Lone Eagle motioned for the lieutenant to follow him.

"There's no danger to Elizabeth?" Lieutenant James asked.

"Only if crazy lady attack with bottle," Lone Eagle answered, and rode toward Ten Sleep.

"What the hell?" Lieutenant James snapped, forgetting himself.

He pursued Lone Eagle into town, right up to the saloon. As he reined in, he heard loud singing coming from the establishment.

Lone Eagle was waiting by the entrance.

Lieutenant James dismounted, then assisted Elizabeth to the street. It was not until then that he noticed the bodies.

"Someone's singing," Elizabeth commented, unaware of the corpses.

"Come," Lieutenant James said, taking her right hand. He led her into the saloon.

The singing stopped. A redhead standing near the bar with a bottle in her left hand almost collapsed at the sight of Elizabeth. The redhead staggered and gripped the bar to steady herself. "You!" she blurted. "The girl from the storeroom!"

"Brooke!" Elizabeth exclaimed. She pulled her right hand loose, and ran over to the woman in the green dress.

"What is goin' on?" Lieutenant James asked. "You know this woman, Elizabeth?"

Elizabeth nodded. "She helped me escape from the Bascombs."

"You're Elizabeth Demming!" Brooke cried happily. "You were kidnapped by the Bascombs!"

# SLAUGHTER AT TEN SLEEP

"Yes. How did you find out?" Elizabeth inquired.

Brooke was clutching the edge of the bar, weaving. Tears filled her eyes. "You're safe! Safe and well! I was so worried about you! So was he!"

"He?" Elizabeth said. "Who are you referring to?"

Brooke, giggling, pretended to shoot imaginary enemies. "Death! I've seen his face!"

"She's drunk," Lieutenant James stated. "She's ravin'."

Elizabeth draped her right arm around Brooke's shoulder. "I need to know about the Bascombs. Are they still in Ten Sleep?"

"Bascombs?" Brooke shook her head. "Don't worry none about those bastards! Ooops! Excuse my mouth!" She tittered.

"You'll get nothin' out of her," Lieutenant James remarked.

"Brooke!" Elizabeth persisted. "The Bascombs! Are the Bascombs still in Ten Sleep?"

Brooke shook her head, her red hair swinging. "Nope! All gone! Yellow bellies! Just us now, honey!"

Lieutenant James walked to the swinging doors and peered outside. Lone Eagle joined him.

"What do you make of those?" Lieutenant James asked nervously, nodded at the figures in the street.

"Dead bluecoats," Lone Eagle said.

"I know that!" Lieutenant James stated impatiently. "But who killed them?"

"Bascombs, maybe," Lone Eagle speculated. "Or the man who makes many widows."

"Preacher? Why would he kill a cavalry patrol?" Lieutenant James said doubtfully. "No. I don't think it was Preacher."

"Whoever kill bluecoats," Lone Eagle stated, "may do same to us."

Lieutenant James anxiously surveyed the street. "Do you think we should ride out? Head for Ten Sleep Canyon now?"

Lone Eagle pointed skyward. The rain was now a steady downpour. The wind was whistling through Ten Sleep. "Not wise to ride in storm. More wind and rain to come. We wait until storm is over."

Elizabeth crossed over to them. "Brooke is close to passing

out," she commented ruefully.

Lieutenant James glanced at the redhead. She was leaning on the bar, her head drooping. "Might be for the best," he remarked. "That lady is goin' to have a whopper of a headache come mornin'."

Brooke looked over at them, grinning. "Come on! Let's whoop it up!"

Elizabeth stared outside. It took her a moment, because of the driving rain and the wind, but she detected the bodies in the street. "Good Lord!" she exclaimed. "Did you know they were there?" she asked Lieutenant James.

James nodded. "Saw 'em when we rode in. I didn't want to worry you so I didn't mention 'em."

"The Bascombs must have killed them," Elizabeth stated with assurance.

"Could be," Lieutenant James agreed. "The Bascombs might have thought the patrol was lookin' for you and ambushed 'em."

"You don't believe the patrol was searching for me?" Elizabeth inquired.

"Doesn't seem likely," Lieutenant James reasoned. "The kidnappers were quite explicit. If they saw any soldiers on their trail, they would kill you. Your father wouldn't risk your life without good cause. I don't know what that patrol was doin' in Ten Sleep, but it must have been somethin' important."

"Lone Eagle will be back," the Crow scout announced, heading for the rear of the saloon.

"Where are you goin'?" Lieutenant James asked.

Lone Eagle glanced over his right shoulder. "Little Britches is hopeless." He kept going.

"Now what do you suppose he meant by that?" Lieutenant James asked.

"Should we bury those poor troopers?" Elizabeth queried.

Lieutenant James watched the rain drench the street. "Not now. Maybe later. Although it might be best to just leave 'em there. The important thing is to get you to your father. General Demming can take care of those men."

A brilliant streak of lightning flashed to the west of Ten Sleep. The saloon seemed to vibrate as thunder shook its foundation.

"My!" Elizabeth declared. "That was close!"

"It's goin' to be a humdinger," Lieutenant James stated.

"Let's have a party!" Brooke called from the bar.

"I should see about tucking her in," Elizabeth said.

"Where?" James asked. "There's no beds in here, and I won't have you crossin' the street in this storm."

"I'm not afraid of getting wet," Elizabeth stated.

"It's not the rain I'm concerned about," Lieutenant James told her.

Lone Eagle came through the rear door, running. He hastened to the front.

"What set your britches on fire?" Lieutenant James inquired, grinning.

Lone Eagle took a deep breath. "More dead bluecoats!"

"What? Where?"

Lone Eagle nodded toward the back of the Tiger Saloon. "Out there. Behind the saloon. Four of them."

Lieutenant James frowned. "Six out front. Four out back. What went on here?"

"I wish we didn't need to spend the night," Elizabeth commented.

Another close lightning bolt illuminated Ten Sleep.

Lone Eagle's eyes narrowed, and he moved to the doors.

"Couldn't we all go to another building?" Elizabeth asked. "I don't feel comfortable in a saloon."

"I suppose we could," Lieutenant James concurred. "First, though, Lone Eagle and I will put our horses in the livery. I don't want to advertise our presence and invite trouble."

"We already have trouble," Lone Eagle stated.

"What? What kind of trouble?" Lieutenant James inquired.

"Riders," Lone Eagle replied.

"Where?" Lieutenant James faced the street.

"Coming into Ten Sleep from the north," Lone Eagle said.

Lieutenant James peered into the night. The rain was falling in sheets. The wind was howling. North of the saloon was a general store and other buildings. There were inky gaps between the structures. "I don't see nothin'," he declared.

"Nor do I," Elizabeth affirmed.

"Look between the buildings," Lone Eagle suggested.

"I still don't see anyone," Lieutenant James said.

"Wait for light in sky," Lone Eagle advised.

They waited. The rain was turning the dusty street into mud.

"Maybe you imagined them," Lieutenant James remarked.

Just then, a bolt of lightning lanced through the sky to the north of Ten Sleep. For a moment the prairie to the north was bathed with a streaking light. And there, clearly visible, was a group of riders.

"I see them!" Elizabeth cried.

"Who could they be?" Lieutenant James asked.

"There are five riders," Lone Eagle informed them, "and they come this way."

Lieutenant James placed his right hand on his holster and glanced at Elizabeth. A burning question branded his brain: What if it was the Bascombs?

# 23

Preacher was two miles to the west of Ten Sleep when the storm started lashing the plain. He rode another mile, and then the full fury of nature's onslaught was unleashed.

It was a lollapalooza.

The rain felt like tiny fingers stabing into Preacher's body. He stopped, debating his next move. Proceeding to the cabin was a foolish notion. In this weather, the journey would be too dangerous; he could easily lose his sense of direction and become disoriented; his horse could stumble in a rut or hole before Preacher even realized it was there; the rain would soak him and his gear, and would turn the ground into a muddy bog; and, the most important consideration, a lone rider on the prairie was a prime attraction for a lightning bolt. Many a horseman had been fried to a crisp in the blink of an eye.

A lightning flash seared the sky to his right.

Preacher squinted against the hammering rain, seeking shelter. A gulch would protect him from the wind and some of the rain, but it would also be prone to a sudden flood. Many of the ravines and gullies, dry ninety-nine percent of the time, were transfigured into violent torrents. Any unsuspecting tinhorn caught in one would be drowned in an instant.

If he couldn't continue to the cabin, and if staying on the

prairie was inviting trouble, only one recourse was available.

Preacher wheeled and rode back toward Ten Sleep.

As Preacher rode, he pondered. He thought of Brooke, of their passion and consummation, and wondered why he couldn't seem to find a woman he'd be willing to settle down with. He liked Brooke, for sure. And there had been others. But there had also been a pattern to his relationships with women, whether romantic or otherwise.

His mother, Matilda, had been killed by raiders on June 2, 1865. His sister, Abby, was later savaged and died in Colorado. Chelsea Glen, the first woman he'd encountered and bedded after leaving Mosby's Rangers, had been shot to death by carpetbaggers. After Chelsea there had been other women, but he'd been engaged in a personal vendetta, in finding and killing every raider responsible for the death of his mother and father.

He'd scoured the west, and he'd done as he'd vowed. One by one, the raiders died. No matter where they had gone, he'd found them. No matter how respectable they might have become, they'd paid for their crimes. Preacher hadn't cared if the bastards were beyond the reach of civil law, they weren't immune to his ideal of justice. They hadn't escaped from Preacher's Law!

And now Preacher was prepared to dispense his particular style of justice again. The Bascombs had abducted an innocent girl, all in the name of greed. They'd terrorized her. Threatened her life. Even if the Bascombs should flee the country, Preacher resolved to track them down. The vermin had to pay for the misery they'd caused decent folks.

A lightning bolt crackled not a hundred yards to the south. The accompanying thunder was instantaneous and deafening.

The stallion shied, nervously jerking his huge head, his eyes wide. Under normal circumstances, the magnificent chestnut responded superbly to Preacher's control. But like most horses, he was easily spooked by lightning and thunder.

Preacher leaned forward and gently stroked his animal. "Easy, boy! Easy!" he said into the stallion's ear.

Preacher hurried toward Ten Sleep. He hoped he was riding in the right direction. The landmarks were gone,

# SLAUGHTER AT TEN SLEEP

obliterated by the wall of rain and the wind. The prairie was shrouded in an ebony mantle. If it wasn't for the lightning periodically illuminating his surroundings, Preacher wouldn't have had the slightest idea where he was.

The damn storm!

Preacher would have to wait it out in Ten Sleep, losing precious time in the bargain. But as soon as it was over, he would ride to the Bascomb's cabin, find Lone Eagle, and get his aid in tracking the Bascombs. Lieutenant James would be left behind for his own safety.

The rain unexpectedly let up, but only for a moment. The wind slackened. It was as if Preacher had ridden into a still pocket at the very heart of the storm. In that fleeting interval, while the prairie was still quiet, a sharp crack sounded from off in the distance, coming from the east, the unmistakable blasting of a long tom, a long gun, one of the heavy caliber rifles preferred by buffalo hunters and many mountain men.

Preacher tensed.

The shot had come from Ten Sleep!

# 24

"What are they doing now?" Elizabeth asked anxiously.

"Just sitting there," Lone Eagle answered. His keen eyes probed the prairie to the north of Ten Sleep. He was waiting for another streak of lightning to provide relief from the darkness.

"I don't like this," Lieutenant James remarked. He surveyed the street, then the interior of the Tiger Saloon. "If it's the Bascombs, we're in for trouble. They'll stop at nothin' to get Elizabeth back."

"Little Britches speaks truth," Lone Eagle agreed.

"What can we do?" Elizabeth inquired.

"Since no one else seems to be in Ten Sleep except us," Lieutenant James said, "we have the entire town to hide in."

"We must hide soon," Lone Eagle stated.

"Why?" Elizabeth questioned him.

Lone Eagle nodded to the north. "They are on the way."

Lieutenant James scrutinized the gap between the general store and another building to its left. A flicker of lightning silhouetted the outlines of five riders moving toward Ten Sleep.

"Let's whoop it up!" yelled Brooke from the bar.

"I plumb forgot about her!" Lieutenant James exclaimed. "Elizabeth! See if you can hush her up!"

## SLAUGHTER AT TEN SLEEP

"Will do." Elizabeth ran toward the bar.

Lone Eagle pointed at the lantern Brooke had lit earlier. "We must not give them edge."

Lieutenant James understood. He hastened to the lantern and quckly blew out the flames.

"Hey! What the hell happened to the light?" Brooke demanded drunkenly.

"Please!" Elizabeth beseeched her. "You must be quiet!"

Brooke took a swig from the bottle in her hand. "Why's that, honey?"

"The Bascombs may be coming," Elizabeth informed her. She found it hard to perceive the other woman in the gloom.

"The Bascombs! Those lily-livered sons of bitches!" Brooke said angrily. "They've got their gall, coming back here!" She slammed the bottle on the bar top.

"Please!" Elizabeth pleaded. "You must hold your tongue! They might hear you!"

"I don't give a damn if they do!" Brooke snapped. She moved from the bar, weaving.

"Where are you going?" Elizabeth asked.

Brooke didn't reply.

Lieutenant James had rejoined Lone Eagle while the women argued. He glanced over his left shoulder. "Quiet down!" he ordered.

The shadowy riders were now on the far side of the general store, coming into town between the general store and the building on its left, directly toward the Tiger Saloon.

"We must leave," Lone Eagle suggested. "Back way."

"Let's go," Lieutenant James said.

The two men started to turn, to hurry across the room, but they stopped as Brooke abruptly barreled past them.

"Where the. . . !" Lieutenant James blurted, and grabbed for her arm.

He missed.

Brooke exited the Tiger Saloon, shoving past the swinging doors and halting outside. The wind made a mess of her red hair, strands whipping her face and flying from her shoulders.

Lieutenant James went to get her.

"No!" Lone Eagle said, gripping Little Britches by his right shoulder and holding fast.

"We can't leave her!" Lieutenant James stated.

"Too late," Lone Eagle declared.

The five black forms emerged from between the general store and the frame building and spread out, forming a line across from the saloon. The rain and the night obscured their features.

Brooke shuffled forward several paces, striving to keep her hair from her face. "Ira!" she shouted. "Is that you?"

"Sure is!" boomed a deep voice. "Evenin', Miss Merriweather!"

Elizabeth came up behind James and Lone Eagle, her head cocked, endeavoring to catch every word.

Brooke moved further from the saloon. "What are you doing back here?" she screamed. "Why don't you leave us be!"

One of the riders, a big man in the center, eased his mount forward several feet. "We can't do that, Miss Merriweather," the giant said.

"The girl ain't here, Ira!" Brooke yelled.

"We know different," Ira responded.

"She ain't here, I tell you!" Brooke shouted defiantly.

"Why, Miss Merriweather! I'm disappointed in you!" Ira bellowed to be heard over the wind and rain. "I always figured you for a lady! But you can't be! Ladies don't lie!"

Brooke raised her fists and shook them. "You lousy bastard! If I was a man, I'd kill you myself!"

Ira ignored her inebriated outburst. He pointed at the blue bellies sprawled in the street. "What happened to them?"

Brooke threw back her head and cackled. "What happened? The same thing as will happen to you if you don't ride out!"

Ira leaned toward her. "I'm not foolin', Miss Merriweather. This is serious business. Who kilt these Yankees?"

"Wouldn't you like to know?" Brooke retorted, laughing.

Ira straightened. "I'm askin' you for the last time, Miss Merriweather, real polite like. We know the folks here lit out. We saw them skedaddle. But we don't know who kilt these blue bellies. We figured they was after us. Who kilt them?"

"Go to hell, Ira!"

Ira looked to his right. "Sherm."

Lieutenant James saw another rider, the one to the right of the big man, move toward the redhead. From the outline of the hat he wore, James guessed this rider was wearing a *sombrero*.

"We must do something!" Elizabeth whispered in an urgent tone. "That's Sherm Bascomb! He'll kill her!"

Lieutenant James glanced from Elizabeth to the street.

"You go out there," Lone Eagle said to him, "they kill you."

Thunder rumbled across the town.

Brooke looked up at the giant. "I thought you were the man who always bragged he'd never murdered a woman or child!"

"I never have," Ira replied.

Brooke pointed at Sherm. "But you turn me over to him, huh? What's the difference?"

Ira wiped water from his dripping beard. "I warned you, Miss Merriweather. And don't play on my sympathy!"

Brooke cackled. "I didn't know you had any!"

"We just came from our cabin," Ira went on. "We found Cy. Dead. Dumped out back."

"Hallelujah!" Brooke shouted. "There's one less Bascomb in the world!"

Ira glared at the redhead. "It's on your shoulders, Miss Merriweather!"

"What is?" Brooke demanded.

"I am," Sherm Bascomb said, angling his horse so its right side was near the woman.

Brooke giggled. "Oh, my! Mercy me! Sherm Bascomb is gunning for me! You sure you can handle an unarmed woman?"

Sherm slowly nodded.

Elizabeth nudged Lieutenant James. "You must help her!"

James took hold of his revolver.

"Wait, Little Britches," Lone Eagle advised.

Brooke took a step toward Sherm. "You bastard! He'll get you! He'll get you, just like he got Cy and Rafe and Rufus!"

Ira Bascomb suddenly dropped to the ground. His boots splashed water and mud as he advanced on Brooke Merriweather. He towered over her, and she cringed. "Rafe and Rufus? They're kilt?"

Brooke straightened. "Yes! And to Hell with their souls!"

"Who?" Ira roared. "Who?"

Brooke stared at each of the Bascombs. Sherm and Boone to her right. Port and Burt to her left. And back to Ira. She knew something they didn't, and in her intoxicated state, her judgments warped by the alcohol, she decided to taunt them, to flaunt her knowledge at their expense. "If you knew who was after you, you'd piss in your pants!"

Ira raised his left hand to strike her.

"Do it!" Brooke shrieked. "Do it! All the time claiming to be such a gentleman! Hypocrite! Crowbait!"

"Who kilt my sons?" Ira shouted.

Brooke tottered backward, almost losing her balance. She steadied herself, tittering. "Who killed Cy?" she baited Ira.

"Yes!" Ira raged.

"Who killed Rafe?"

"Yes!"

"Who killed Rufus?"

Brooke clapped her hands, delighted at the fury reflected on Ira's face. "I'll tell you, Ira! Just so I can see you turn yellow and light out! It was Death! The Widow Maker! J.D. Preacher!"

Ira stiffened. "Preacher? Here?"

"That's right!" Brooke gloated. "He's after you for stealing the general's daughter! He'll kill you! You and all your stinking brood!"

"Enough!" Sherm cried. "How would you know so much about the Widow Maker?"

Brooke laughed. "Because he and I spent some time together, little man! And after seeing what Preacher had to offer, I do mean *little* man!"

Sherm shot her. His right Navy Colt streaked out and boomed, and Brooke was hit in the forehead. Her head snapped back, her eyes fluttering, and she toppled to the mud.

"No!" Elizabeth wailed.

Lieutenant James pulled his gun and pushed through the doors. He aimed at the Bascomb with the *sombrero* and squeezed the trigger, but his hand was unsteady. He saw the *sombrero* jerk from Sherm's head, and then Sherm was firing both Colts, splintering the wall inches from the lieutenant's left shoulder. James sighted for another try, but strong hands grabbed him and pulled him inside the saloon.

The Bascombs were diving for cover, shooting as they ran.

Slugs bit into the swinging doors and the outside wall.

Inside, huddled to the right of the doorway, Lone Eagle waved Lieutenant James and Elizabeth toward the rear of the saloon. "Run! Lone Eagle will delay them!"

Lieutenant James gripped Elizabeth's left wrist and raced to the back door.

Lone Eagle commenced peppering the street with his Winchester.

"Come on!" Lieutenant James yelled. "That'll hold them for a spell."

Lone Eagle dashed over to them. "We must hide!"

"But where?" Elizabeth asked.

"Not here!" Lone Eagle replied.

Lieutenant James shoved the rear door open, and they ran into the stinging rain and the gusting wind.

"Which way?" Elizabeth shouted.

Lieutenant James turned to the left, sticking to the rear wall of the saloon. He hurried to the end of the wall, to the space between the saloon and the next building. Cautiously, he peeked into the narrow alley.

It appeared to be empty.

Lieutenant James hauled Elizabeth after him as he crossed the alley and reached the next structure, a frame building.

Lone Eagle stayed with them, constantly glancing behind them, covering their flight.

Lightning speared the sky to the south.

"Hurry!" Elizabeth goaded, looking back. She dreaded falling into the Bascomb's clutches again. The sight of Brooke Merriweather lying in the mud, with a bloody hole in her forehead, was one Elizabeth would never forget.

Lieutenant James gazed into the next alley.

Nothing.

They dashed across the opening.

A shot sounded from the street end of the alley as a flash of flame spurted in their direction.

Lieutenant James felt a slug penetrate his right shoulder. He was spun around by the force of the impact, losing his hold on Elizabeth. He tripped and went down onto his knees.

Lone Eagle levered several rounds up the alley, then reached down and wrapped his right arm around Little Britches' waist. He lifted, propelling the sagging officer to the cover of the next building.

Elizabeth was at James' side. "You're hurt!"

Lieutenant James leaned on the wall. "Just a scratch," he told her. But the wound didn't fell like a scratch. His shoulder burned, like someone had buried a branding iron in his body. He tried to grin. "I'll be fine."

"Sure," Lone Eagle interjected. "Come!" He supporting the lieutenant, hastening up to a door in the middle of the building.

Elizabeth tried the latch. "It's locked!"

Lone Eagle drew in his right leg and kicked. The door jamb splintered, and the door swung inward and crashed against a hall wall. He assisted Little Britches over the threshold, aided by Elizabeth. "Close the door!" he instructed her when they were inside.

Elizabeth pushed the door shot, managing to wedge it against the shattered jamb. "They'll bust through this, easy," she commented.

"Can you walk?" Lone Eagle asked Little Britches.

Lieutenant James nodded. "Lead the way." He realized he was still holding his revolver in his right hand, and transferred it to his left.

Lone Eagle led them down a gloomy hallway to a living room.

"We're in someone's house!" Elizabeth exclaimed, as if the intrusion into a private residence was worse than the fate awaiting them outdoors.

A large window fronted Ten Sleep's main street.

"Stay down!" Lone Eagle warned them. He dropped into a squat, then scurried over to the window.

Lieutenant James and Elizabeth crouched at the end of the hallway.

"We'll see you out of this safely," Lieutenant James said, keeping his attention focused on the back door.

Elizabeth touched his right cheek. "Whatever happens," she said softly, "I'll always be in your debt."

Lieutenant James forced a grin. "Does this mean our date is on?"

Elizabeth nodded.

"Shhhhh!" Lone Eagle whispered. He carefully peered over the window sill at the street. All he could see was the rainstorm in all its elemental turbulence.

# SLAUGHTER AT TEN SLEEP

"Any sign of them?" Lieutenant James asked in a hushed tone.

Lone Eagle shook his head. He bit his lower lip, concentrating on their predicament. Leaving Ten Sleep on foot and waiting for the rain to stop and the Bascombs to leave would be best. But could Little Britches hold out with his wound? Or would the gunshot become infected? A horse would be nice, but the Bascombs would have driven their mounts off or hidden them. Staying in the house would shelter them from the downpour, but they would be boxed in if the Bascombs discovered them. He turned and crawled over to Lieutenant James and Elizabeth.

"This is a fine fix we're in," Elizabeth said. "And all because of me!"

"Was it your fault you were kidnapped?" Lieutenant James asked. "If you need to blame anyone for this, then blame the Bascombs."

"We blame someone later," Lone Eagle said. "We must escape Bascombs first."

"How will we do that?" Elizabeth wanted to know.

"I have an idea," Lieutenant James declared.

"What is it?" Elizabeth queried eagerly.

"The Bascombs won't allow us to leave alive," Lieutenant James said. "At least, not Lone Eagle and myself. They'll keep searchin' for you, Elizabeth, until they find you. They're most likely goin' from buildin' to buildin' right this minute." He paused and gazed at both of them. "We can't let them take Elizabeth again! I propose to create a diversion, allowin' the two of you to sneak out of Ten Sleep."

"We won't leave you!" Elizabeth stated.

"You have no choice," Lieutenant James responded. "I'd go too, but I couldn't move very fast with this shoulder. No," He stared at Lone Eagle, "It'll be up to you. You understand?"

Lone Eagle nodded, smiling. "Little Britches more man than Lone Eagle thought."

"I won't leave you!" Elizabeth vowed.

Lieutenant James tenderly stroked his left thumb under her chin. "You must."

Elizabeth opened her mouth to object.

"Hear me out," Lieutenant James cut her off. He studied

her lovely features as he addressed her. "I know we hardly know each other. But I also know how I feel inside whenever I look at you. I left my post to come find you. If anythin' were to happen to you, I wouldn't want to go on. This probably sounds silly to you, Elizabeth, considerin' we're virtual strangers and all, but I reckon I'm fallin' in love with you. If I ain't already."

He paused. "You *must* go with Lone Eagle. The Bascombs will find us here, sooner or later. With my clipped wing, I couldn't very well protect you and watch out for myself at the same time. But I can, and I will, draw the Bascombs away from you so Lone Eagle can take you to safety. I admire your loyalty, Elizabeth. But you must go. For my sake."

Elizabeth took his left hand in hers, gun and all, and squeezed. "You take care, you hear?"

Lieutenant James nodded. "I will. Now go. Before the Bascombs find us."

Lone Eagle rose and moved toward the back door.

"Go with him," Lieutenant James urged her. "I'll be goin' out the front."

Elizabeth took several steps, then paused. "Oh my God! I just realized I don't even know your first name?"

Lieutenant James grinned. "William. But all my friends call me Will."

Elizabeth smiled, worry etched in her expression. "I expect to see you again, Will James."

Lieutenant James nodded. "The good Lord willin'."

"Come!" Lone Eagle prompted.

Elizabeth cast an apprehensive look at the youthful officer, then hastened to the rear door.

Lone Eagle cautiously opened the door. He risked a quick peek to the right and the left, then departed, bearing to the left.

Elizabeth stayed on the Crow scout's heels.

Lieutenant James sighed as he struggled to a standing posture. He could still feel the lingering sensation of Elizabeth's fingers touching the knuckles of his left hand. Finally! A woman he could love! A woman who was interested in him! He walked to the front door, smirking at the irony of it all. He'd found a reason to live when he was, quite possibly, on the verge of dying. Didn't seem fair, somehow.

The thunderstorm was continuing to pound Ten Sleep with wind and rain.

Perfect. The storm would provide the cover he'd so desperately need if he was to carry this lunacy off! Lieutenant James tried the latch, found it unlocked. He eased the door open an inch, then two.

Rain splattered onto the floor at his feet.

He tightened his grip on his revolver, then slid from the house, keeping his back flush with the front window. Eyes and ears straining, he moved to his left, to the west, toward the saloon.

Lightning sparkled. Thunder crashed.

Lieutenant James reached the end of the house. He peered into the alley from which he'd been ambushed. Nothing stirred.

Where were the Bascombs?

Lieutenant James ran to the next building. His boots almost slipped on a slick spot. He regained his balance and halted, breathing heavily. His right shoulder was sheer torment, disrupting his concentration. He shook his head, trying to shake off the pain.

The motion saved his life.

A long gun on the opposite side of the street boomed, and the wood less than an inch from Lieutenant James' right ear dissolved into flying shards. He felt a stinging in his right cheek, and then he was in motion, running now, making for the Tiger Saloon. He clumsily pointed his gun in the general direction of the sniper and fired.

Another Bascomb opened up from across the street, this one using a pistol, blasting three shots in succession.

Lieutenant James heard the slugs thud into the building behind him and suddenly another alley appeared ahead, the alley before the saloon, and he raced across it. Or attempted to do so. Before he could reach the saloon, a hurtling form, rushing pell-mell toward the street from the alley's depths, collided with him, sending both of them sprawling.

Lieutenant James grimaced as he landed on his injured shoulder. He came up onto his knees, catching a fleeting glimpse of the youngest Bascomb doing the same not a foot away, and he lashed out with the barrel of his revolver, slamming it into the youngest Bascomb's face, breaking his nose. His foe screeched and frantically lunged for the alley on his hands and knees, blood spilling from his crushed nostrils.

Lieutenant James surged to his feet and hustled toward the saloon doors, hunched over because of the excruciating agony in his shoulder. He reached the swinging doors and started to shove them open. A volley erupted from the other side of the street, three or four guns all at once. The swinging doors were struck again and again, the wood chipping and splintering. Lieutenant James was almost inside when a slug ripped through his right thigh, causing him to cry out, and he was hurled to the floor.

"They're killing him!" Elizabeth wailed.

They were behind the last building on the extreme east end of Ten Sleep. Another thirty feet and they would be clear of the town and on the prairie, where the possibilities of locating a safe hiding place were endless.

"We must go!" Lone Eagle, in the lead, told her. "Come!"

Elizabeth turned, about to return into Ten Sleep.

Lone Eagle seized her right wrist and held fast. "Come! Or all Little Britches does is wasted!"

Lieutenant James crawled to the nearest chair and used it to brace his body as he rose. His left leg supported his weight. It had to, because he couldn't stand to apply any pressure on his right foot.

"He's in the Tiger!" someone shouted outside.

Lieutenant James hopped toward the bar. His right leg felt damp, and something was trickling over his knee. Blood. He was losing a lot of blood. He shut the fact from his mind as he reached the north end of the bar and dropped behind it.

"You two take the back!" yelled the voice outside.

They were hemming him in. Lieutenant James fumbled with his revolver, extracting the spent cartridges. He clutched at his belt pouch, his fingers shaking, and removed the ammunition he needed.

There was a loud thump from the rear of the saloon.

Lieutenant James grit his teeth as he reloaded. He cocked the hammer and slowly rose, his left leg trembling, his right elbow pressed against the inner shelves on the bar as a brace.

Something—or someone—made a scraping noise, coming from the direction of the swinging doors.

The Bascombs were closing in.

Lieutenant James inhaled, then came erect, his gun extended, and he fired at a cluster of moving shadows near the swinging doors.

Instantly, bright bursts rent the saloon and its walls rocked from gunshot after gunshot.

Lieutenant James was caught in a crossfire, with slugs smacking into the bar all around him. He pivoted, aiming at a bulky form near the back door, and squeezed the trigger.

The mirror behind the bar fractured and collapsed. Bottles were shattering and tumbling to the floor by the dozens.

Lieutenant James faced front again, sighting. But before he could shoot a third time, his chest was kicked by a Missouri mule and he was flung against the wall, crashing into a row of whiskey bottles. He slumped to the floor, feeling dizzy.

"I got the son of a bitch!" a man shouted triumphantly.

Lieutenant James frowned. He'd wanted to give a better accounting of himself. He attempted to rise onto his elbows, but his arms were unwilling to cooperate. His right shoulder and leg hurt, but, to his great surprise, his chest didn't. He wondered why as his eyelids closed.

"Let me go!" Elizabeth screamed.

Lone Eagle had his hands full. He held the Winchester in his right and the general's bobcat of a daughter in his left. They were mere yards from cover. "We must go!" he told her, striving to yank her into the brush.

"We can't just leave him!" Elizabeth fumed.

"You agreed!" Lone Eagle reminded her.

They could hear the gunfire coming from Ten Sleep.

"I've changed my mind!" Elizabeth protested. "Take me back!"

"No! We go!" Lone Eagle exerted all of his strength and pulled her toward the nearest vegetation.

Elizabeth dug in her heels and wrenched her body away from Lone Eagle. The rain worked in her favor. Her wrist, soaked by the rain, was slippery, too slippery to be grasped securely.

Lone Eagle, straining, his torso leaning forward, felt his

hand slide and lose its grip, and before he could grab her again his momentum carried him onto his knees.

Elizabeth bolted, darting into Ten Sleep.

Lone Eagle never hesitated. He rose and ran after the girl, her white dress enabling him to keep her in sight as she ducked into an alley and headed for the main street.

Tonight was a night for loco white women!

Lone Eagle pursued the girl into the alley. His keen eyesight enabled him to carefully circumvent a pile of wooden crates, and then he was out of the alley and on Ten Sleep's main street.

Elizabeth Demming was racing headlong down the middle of the muddy street, heedless of the danger, oblivious to everything except finding Lieutenant James.

Lone Eagle sprinted after her. He scanned both sides of the street, alert for the slightest movement. Incredibly, they were almost to the saloon before the Bascombs appeared.

Elizabeth was ten yards from the swinging doors, her hair plastered to her head and shoulders by the rain, her dress a sorry shade of light brown from the knees down, when the doors to the Tiger Saloon opened and Port Bascomb strode into view.

The rain had slowed, and the wind was commencing to taper off.

Elizabeth spotted Port and froze in her tracks.

Lone Eagle, eight yards behind the girl, moved to his left, seeking a line of fire unobstructed by the girl's body.

Port Bascomb was grinning and saying something to someone in the doorway when he spied their quarry. "It's her!" he bellowed. "The Demming bitch!" He sprang toward her.

Elizabeth seemed to have grown roots.

Lone Eagle raised his Winchester and fired, a hasty shot but effective nonetheless.

Port Bascomb grunted as he was hit in the left side. The slug dug a furrow in his flesh and tore his shirt open, but the wound wasn't fatal. He twisted and sprawled on the ground, clawing at his Smith and Wesson.

Lone Eagle ran up to Elizabeth and looped his left arm around her slim waist. He spun, hurrying to the right, making for the general store.

Port Bascomb was having difficulty holding his Smith and

Wesson. His thick fingers were so coated with mud, he couldn't maintain his hold on the grips.

Lone Eagle was five-feet from the general store when another of the Bascombs, the one with the *sombrero*—the *sombrero* he must have retrieved after Lieutenant James shot it from his head—came through the swinging doors.

Sherm held his Navy Colts low and steady, and he cut loose with both guns, blasting away as the Indian and the girl angled toward the general store door, blasting again as they reached the door, and blasting a third time as the Indian plowed into the door with his left shoulder. Both the Indian and the girl plunged out of sight.

Port scrambled to his feet and, keeping stooped over, sped into the saloon.

Sherm backed through the swinging doors.

On the floor of the general store, Lone Eagle rolled onto his back and felt along his abdomen with his left hand.

Elizabeth, stunned, was on her right side next to him. She placed her palms on the hardwood floor and rose on her hands and knees. "I'm sorry!" she blurted. "I wasn't thinking!"

He raised his left hand, blood dripping from his fingers.

"You've been hit!" Elizabeth exclaimed.

Lone Eagle grunted. "Are you hit?" he asked.

Elizabeth glanced down at herself. "No. I'm fine. But my dress is a mess."

"Lone Eagle not so lucky," he remarked, sitting up.

"How bad is it?" Elizabeth inquired. Her eyes widened as she beheld the large reddish circle spreading over his buckskin shirt.

"Bad," Lone Eagle said. "Look outside. Tell Lone Eagle what is there."

Elizabeth crept to the doorway, staying to the right of the jamb. Outside, the rain had tapered to a drizzle, and the wind was a mere breeze. The storm was stopping. She could see the front of the saloon, but nothing of the Bascombs. "I don't see them," she whispered.

"We must find other way out," Lone Eagle stated. He slowly stood, using the Winchester stock to prop him erect.

"There's a window in the storeroom," Elizabeth informed him. "I busted it out last night. We can climb out there."

"Take me," Lone Eagle instructed her.

Elizabeth hurried around the counter and past the curtain. She moved down the hall to the storeroom door, finding it locked. She remembered Brooke taking a key from under the small barrel in the corner, and promptly did likewise.

Lone Eagle stood near the curtain, watching the front door.

Elizabeth inserted the key and unlocked the storeroom. "It's open!" she announced.

Lone Eagle shuffled to her side. He looked up at the window and grimaced. "Lone Eagle maybe stay here."

"What?" Elizabeth stared at the crimson stain on his shirt. "You can do it! I'll give you a boost!"

They walked to the back wall. Lone Eagle stepped over a pile of canned goods and gazed upward. Two wooden shelves served as a makeshift ladder. There was a space between the shelves, as if a third one might be missing. His right toe nudged a hard object, and he glanced down to discover the missing shelf.

"You go first," Elizabeth said.

"You," Lone Eagle replied, motioning toward the window.

"I can push you up," Elizabeth told him.

"You pull Lone Eagle up," he corrected her.

Elizabeth placed her right foot on the lowest shelf, and reached overhead for the next one. She scaled the wall with ease. Surprisingly, Brooke hadn't bothered to cover the broken window. Elizabeth was outside in moments. She turned and poked her head inside. "Come on! Take my hand." She extended her right arm as far as she could reach.

"Take this," Lone Eagle said, and elevated the Winchester.

Elizabeth gripped the rifle and pulled it out the window, leaving the gun on the ground as she offered her arm again. "Now you."

Lone Eagle stoically resisted the torture in his stomach. He put his right moccasin on the lowest shelf and shoved off, his arms above his head. His hands almost grabbed the window sill, missing by inches. Elizabeth grasped his right wrist and heaved. He managed to clasp the sill, his body suspended, and raised his right leg and caught his foot on the highest shelf.

"We're going to do it!" Elizabeth said, elated.

# SLAUGHTER AT TEN SLEEP

Lone Eagle felt his hands starting to slip, but then Elizabeth took hold of his other wrist, braced her feet against the outer edge of the window, and yanked. Lone Eagle scraped his abdomen as his head and shoulders went through the window. Light rain dropped on his face.

"Keep coming!" Elizabeth goaded him.

Between them, Lone Eagle was able to crawl from the storeroom. He rose, picking up his Winchester.

"What now?" Elizabeth asked.

"Must leave Ten Sleep," Lone Eagle stated. "Hurry." He waved her to the west, toward the livery stable.

Elizabeth ran to the corner of the general store and scrutinized the next alley.

"Any Bascombs?" Lone Eagle inquired.

"I don't see any," Elizabeth whispered. The rain had almost ceased, and she found it a lot easier to see.

"Go to livery," Lone Eagle directed her. "Might find horses. Then ride to find your father."

"Do you think the Bascombs killed Will?" Elizabeth asked.

"Little Britches can handle himself," Lone Eagle said. He nudged her to proceed.

Elizabeth headed across the alley, Lone Eagle right behind her.

"Injun!"

The harsh shout came from the street end of the alley. Elizabeth whirled, shocked to behold Sherm and Boone Bascomb framed in the mouth of the alley, Sherm with his ivory handled Colts, Boone with his needle gun pressed to his right shoulder.

"No!" Elizabeth screamed, trying to throw her body between Lone Eagle and the Bascomb brothers.

Elizabeth didn't make it.

Lone Eagle brought his Winchester up, going for a snap shot, but Boone Bascomb was faster.

Boone's big Springfield sounded louder than the thunder in the confines of the alley.

Lone Eagle took the slug in the center of his face, on the tip of his nose. The force of the .50-70 lifted the Crow scout from his feet and sent him crashing to the damp grass six-feet from the alley.

"No!" Elizabeth ran to Lone Eagle's side.

Lone Eagle quivered once, then was still. His nose was gone, replaced by a jagged hole. His eyes were open, glazed. A sizeable portion of his skull, brains, and blood, had been blown from his head and scattered about the grass.

Elizabeth felt tears form in her tired eyes. "Oh! I'm so sorry!" she said softly.

"Ain't this sweet!" Sherm barked, not a foot to her rear, and before she could turn on him, his arms encircled her waist and began dragging her down the alley.

"You . . . you sons of bitches!" Elizabeth raged, kicking and flailing.

Boone Bascomb was waiting for them, calmly reloading hs needle gun.

"You bastard!" Elizabeth fumed, hatred distorting her features. "You'll pay for what you've done! Every one of you! You deserve to burn in hell! If it's the last act I ever commit, I'll see all of you dead!"

"Oh?" Boone smirked. "Who's goin' to kill us? You?"

Boone and Sherm laughed.

# 25

Ira Bascomb was in good spirits. The best he'd felt in days. They'd recovered the girl! Their scheme to obtain the gold could be carried out! And the rest of his boys were still alive! The news about Rafe and Rufus, coming as it did on the heels of finding Cy's body behind the cabin, had shaken him.

He was standing at the bar in the Tiger Saloon, serving himself. Several lanterns had been lit. He swallowed a glass of red eye in one gulp, scanning the saloon, swelled with pride at how well his sons had performed.

Burt was seated at a table to Ira's left, a wet cloth over his busted nose. The general's daughter sat at the same table, her arms folded across her bosom, glaring at everyone and everything. Port was at a table in front of Ira, examining his wound for the umpteenth time. Sherm and Boone were standing at the north end of the bar, drinking and chuckling, eyeing Elizabeth Demming.

Ira poured another drink and raised the glass. "We done it, boys! That gold is as good as ours! Let's drink to General Demming!"

"And the Confederacy!" Sherm added.

"The Confederate State of America!" Boone chimed in.

The Bascombs, all except for Burt, tipped their glasses.

"To your deaths!" Elizabeth belatedly mentioned.

Port glanced at her. "That's hardly a proper attitude, missy. We ain't harmed you, have we?"

"You're all polecats!" Elizabeth snapped.

Ira stared at the body of the Yankee officer lying on the floor behind the bar. "Another lousy blue belly dies. So what? After what they did to the South, every Yankee dog deserves to die!"

"So do you!" Elizabeth retorted.

Ira sighed. "Enough of this prattle! Burt, go fetch our horses from the livery."

"Can't Port do it?" Burt asked, his words muffled by the cloth on his nose. "I hurt, Pa."

"Hurtin' is part of life, boy," Ira declared. "A real man don't bellyache about it! Now go when I tell you!"

Burt frowned. He rose and slowly walked toward the swinging doors.

"Don't fret none, Burt," Sherm teased him. "Who knows? A busted nose could be an improvement on you!"

Boone, Port and Sherm cackled.

Burt paused, angrily gazing at each of them. "You wouldn't think it was so funny if it'd happened to you!"

"I was hit, wasn't I?" Port stated. "You don't hear me whinin', do you?"

"Fetch those horses!" Ira bellowed. "We'd best leave Ten Sleep before the army shows up."

"Or someone else," Elizabeth casually commented.

"Like who?" Ira demanded.

"You know who," Elizabeth mocked him.

Ira knew, but he refused to acknowledge the fact. "No, I don't. Who?"

"I think she means him!" Burt exclaimed. He was standing at the swinging doors.

"Who?" Ira absently asked.

"The *hombre* in the street!" Burt declared.

The Bascombs flocked to the doorway, Port grabbing Elizabeth's left arm and dragging her after him.

"I'll be damned!" Ira said in amazement.

He was waiting for them in the middle of the street. The man in black. Ira had heard the description a dozen times. Black britches. White shirt. Black frock coat. Black broad brimmed hat. Black boots. The man Ira had wanted to meet for years.

"The Widow Maker!" Burt declared.

"What do we do, Pa?" Boone inquired, hefting his needle gun.

"Let me take him," Sherm said, his hands on his Colts.

"If it's all the same to you," Port stated, "I'll stay here with missy."

Ira pondered for a moment. "Burt will stay with Miss Demming."

"Let me take him, Pa," Sherm repeated eagerly.

"Not this one, son," Ira said.

"Why not?" Sherm responded. "I figure I can gun him down, easy."

"Maybe. Maybe not," Ira said. "But this is a family affair. We'll all do him in."

"He has it comin'," Boone mentioned. "For what he did!"

"He looks like he's on the prod," Port stated nervously.

"So?" Ira rejoined. "He can't gun us all. Not us all, he can't."

"Hellfire! I aim to cut him down before he can draw his equalizer!" Sherm boasted.

Ira glanced at Sherm. "Don't be takin' the Widow Maker for granted, boy. He's a *brujo* with a six-gun."

"He may be a wizard with an iron," Sherm affirmed, "but so am I."

Elizabeth snickered contemptuously. "Talk is cheap!" she taunted them.

Ira squared his shoulders. "Let's go. Burt, you stay with Miss Demming."

"Will do, Pa," Burt said.

Ira shoved past the swinging doors. He took three paces and stopped, studying the man in black. Sherm moved to Ira' right, while Port and Boone angled to his left.

"So you're the Widow Maker?" Ira said sarcastically.

"And you're the Bascombs," Preacher replied.

"Yep. I'm Ira," Ira informed him. "These are my boys. Sherm and Port and Boone."

Preacher appraised his opposition. The one called Sherm, the evident pistoleer, would be the quickest on the draw. Port, the heavy one, the slowest. The one named Boone was muscular, rangy. The needle gun Boone carried only contained one shot. But one shot was all the man in buckskins would need. The giant, Ira, probably relied more on his prodigious strength than his six shooter. So when the time came to make smoke, the fastest Bascomb, Sherm, would be the one Preacher went for first.

"We've been lookin' forward to meetin' you," Ira said.

"Why?" Preacher asked. He knew the Bascombs would size him up for a spell, then go for their guns. They'd want to try and catch him off guard.

"You don't know?" Ira responded.

"No," Preacher said. He saw no need to mention his speculation concerning the raider he'd shot in Missouri.

"I'm plumb disappointed," Ira stated. "I figured the great J.D. Preacher would be able to put two and two together! Doesn't our last name tell you somethin'?"

"Should it?" Preacher countered.

Ira's face reddened. "Damn right it should! Bascomb! You met a man called Bascomb once before! 'Course, it was his middle name. Andrew Bascomb Posey. That name familiar to you, Preacher?"

Preacher nodded. "One of the murdering bastards responsible for the deaths of my father and mother."

Ira's eyes narrowed. "That murderin' bastard, as you call him, was my brother! And you kilt him! You shot him in the back, you bushwhackin' coyote!"

"It was a fair fight," Preacher said. "I called him and he threw down on me, and I killed him just like I'm going to kill you."

"All four of us?" Ira retorted skeptically.

"I've already killed three Bascombs," Preacher remarked. "Four, if you count your brother. What's four or five more?"

He could see the head of another man, it had to be another Bascomb, and of a woman with long black hair, it had to be Elizabeth Demming, visible just above the swinging doors to the saloon.

"I heard 'bout what you did to the twins," Ira said bitterly.

"You shouldn't have sent boys to do a man's job," Preacher declared.

"I didn't send 'em," Ira disclosed. "They went after you on their own accord. I'd of never let them go up against you alone." He paused. "The twins was my pride and joy! I was hopin' to spare 'em from bein' wanted by the law. I wasn't

## SLAUGHTER AT TEN SLEEP 169

goin' to involve 'em in this gold business." He surveyed the dark street. "Why do you think I moved out here to this Godforsaken neck of the woods?"

"Because it became too hot for you back East," Preacher deduced. "Because the law was after you for one reason or another. So you up and skedaddled to the Wyoming Territory. You changed your last name from Posey to Bascomb to hide your identity. You took the name Bascomb in honor of your brother. How am I doing so far?"

Ira nodded. "You're doin' fine."

Preacher continued, "you settled near Ten Sleep, far from the nearest sheriff or marshal or army post. You tried to avoid attracting attention. But then you learned about the stashed gold, and you decided this was your big break. You concocted your loco plan to have the army find the gold for you. Am I still doing fine?"

"I take it back," Ira said. "You ain't as dumb as I first figured."

"Now that the pleasantries are out of the way," Preacher said icily, "let's settle it."

Sherm took a step forward, grinning. "You left somethin' out, Preacher."

"What?" Preacher responded suspiciously.

"You ain't seen her yet?" Sherm asked cockily.

Preacher's brow creased. What was the gunny talking about? The rain had ceased, but the sky was still overcast with dark clouds. Except for the light coming from the saloon, Ten Sleep was buried in an inky murk.

"Look to your left, Preacher," Sherm said, then licked his lips.

Preacher risked a hasty glance. He'd entered Ten Sleep from the west, and had left the stallion behind the livery. The Bascombs had been easy to find; they'd occupied the only illuminated building in the entire town. He'd seen the bodies littering the main street, but they hadn't rated special attention; they were the bodies of the six troopers he'd killed. His mind automatically counted them now, and he was puzzled when he reached the seventh corpse. The light from the saloon served to outline the Bascombs, but it only extended to about the middle of the street. Preacher had deliberately stopped at the edge of the light. There was just enough light for the Bascombs to see him, but not enough for them to see every detail. He squinted at the seventh body, covered with mud head to toe, and recognition slowly dawned. Her red hair, spattered by the mud and the rain was now brown. Her arms and legs were encased in the muck. She was lying face down, brown dots coating her red dress.

It was Brooke Merriweather.

Preacher glanced up at the Bascombs.

"It was me, Preacher!" Sherm gloated. "I did it! Shot her just like I'm goin' to shoot you!"

Preacher tensed expectantly.

The Bascombs waited on Sherm to make their play. They realized they held the edge. Preacher would be forced to go for Sherm first, and in the time it would take Preacher to draw and fire at Sherm, the others would cut loose. Ira had been right, and his sons knew it. There was no way Preacher could get them all. They were experienced gunhands. They might be slower than the Widow Maker, but even a slow gunman could kill a skilled shootist with one accurate shot if the shootist's attention was diverted.

Like now.

Preacher anticipated their strategy. These men weren't raw troopers with bulky revolvers and flap-covered holsters. They were seasoned professional killers. And they deserved to be treated with supreme respect.

Sherm Bascomb licked his thin lips again. His mind filled with images of the glory he would receive after he downed Preacher. J.D. Preacher ranked right up there with Wild Bill Hickok as one of the preeminent man-killers in the West. Whoever gunned down the Widow Maker would achieve instant fame and lasting immortality. Sherm thought it was only fitting for the honor to be bestowed upon him. Never once did he entertain the notion Preacher might beat him.

The Widow Maker stood in the street, his arms at his sides.

Sherm grinned, threw back his head and laughed, and when he gazed at the street again, at the man in black, he was ready. His hands were a blur as he jerked out his prized Colts. The barrels came out and around, his fingers tightening on the triggers, when his dreams of glory were rudely shattered by the booming of Preacher's hip gun.

# SLAUGHTER AT TEN SLEEP

Sherm felt an intense burning in his chest as he was flung backwards into the front wall of the saloon. He still managed to squeeze off two shots, but they were both low and Preacher was already in motion, moving to Sherm's right. Sherm saw the man in black fire again, and Sherm's head was slammed into the wall. His final conscious thought, before he staggered forward and toppled into the mud, summed up his sentiments exactly: Damn! I missed!

Preacher fired again as he dived to the left, and the fat Bascomb spun around and dropped.

Ira had drawn his iron and flattened, and he aimed and squeezed the trigger with calculated deliberation.

Something stung Preacher's right shoulder, but he ignored it as he rolled and rose up on his left knee.

Boone Bascomb had taken cover at the corner of the saloon. The barrel of the needle gun poked around the corner.

Preacher threw himself backwards, landing in the mud as the needle gun went off. The shot missed, and before Boone could reload and try again, Preacher vaulted to his feet and darted into the general store. A volley smacked into the walls on both sides of the doorway. Preacher ducked to the left. He crouched and peered around the jamb, just in time to see Boone and Ira, holding Port between them, duck into the saloon.

It was a temporary standoff.

Preacher reloaded the spent chambers in his hip gun, then took stock. His clothes were caked with mud. And his right shoulder had been creased. Otherwise, he was fine.

There was a commotion inside the saloon. Loud voices. The lanterns were suddenly extinguished.

Preacher nodded. The Bascombs wouldn't make the same mistake twice. They should have damped the lights before they walked out to face him.

"Preacher!"

Preacher moved to the window and carefully peeked out the bottom corner.

"Preacher!" It was Ira Bascomb. "You hear me?"

"What do you want?" Preacher called.

"I'm through playin' fair with you!" Ira yelled. "You kilt Sherm! And Port has a nasty head wound!"

Preacher didn't bother to respond.

"We still got the ace in the hole!" Ira shouted. "We got you outnumbered! And we got the girl!"

Preacher frowned.

"You listenin' to me?" Ira sked.

"I'm listening!" Preacher answered.

"Good. Then here's the way it is! You throw out your iron and come out with your arms reachin' for the sky, or, so help me, I'll shoot the girl!"

Preacher ran to the counter, then down the hallway to the storeroom. It rquired but a moment for him to scale the rear wall and clamber out the window. He could hear Ira bawling at the top of his lungs.

"Did you hear me, Preacher?"

Preacher raced to the east, keeping close to the buildings. He passed two structures, then cut down an alley to the main street.

"You'd best answer me!" Ira was threatening the empty general store.

Preacher sprinted across the street, hoping the Bascombs were all focusing their attention on the general store. He reached the far side and continued down an alley until he was behind the buildings lining the south side of the main street.

"I'll count to three!" Ira warned.

Preacher sped toward the rear door of the saloon.

"If you don't show, I'll send the girl back to the general in little pieces!"

Preacher was one building away from the saloon.

"One!" Ira counted.

Preacher reached the last alley before the saloon.

"Two!"

Preacher came to an abrupt stop next to the back door. He cautiously eased the door open and looked inside.

"Do you think I'm joshin'?" Ira Bascomb shouted.

He was standing at the swinging doors. Boone Bascomb was next to his father. Port Bascomb, blood dripping from a furrow on the right side of his head, stood at the front window. The last Bascomb, a kid with blond hair, was holding onto Elizabeth Bascomb, clutching her left wrist in his right hand, both of them standing behind Ira.

"This is it!" Ira roared.

All the Bascombs were heeled, Boone with his big needle

gun, the others with revolvers in their hands.

"Three!" Ira finished his count. He glanced at the empty street. "I reckon the Widow Maker cares more about his own hide than he does about what happens to you."

Preacher slid into the saloon. The Bascombs were all facing front, vaguely visible in the dim interior.

Ira cocked his Remington. "Sorry, Miss Demming. I ain't never kilt no woman before, but I reckon there's a first time for everything." He began to turn.

Preacher was thirty-feet from the Bascombs. He intended to move closer. The nearer he was to the Bascombs, the more startled they would be, the less time they would have to react. He took one more step.

The floorboard creaked.

The kid with the blond hair twisted, looking over his right shoulder, his mouth dropping open in astonishment. "Pa!" he screeched, and raised his Dragoon.

Preacher shot the kid between his blue eyes.

Burt Bascomb stumbled backwards, into his father, knocking Ira through the swinging doors.

Port Bascomb whirled and snapped off a hasty shot. He missed.

Preacher didn't. His forty-four forty belched lead, and Port was hit high on the right temple. The shot twirled Port to the right, and he tripped over his own feet as he stumbled into the front window, his momentum and bulk hurling him through the glass in a great crashing spray of jagged fragments.

Boone Bascomb never bothered to fire. He crouched and leaped, springing under the swinging doors and rolling to safety outside.

The saloon became deathly still.

Preacher ran up to Elizabeth Demming. "Are you all right?" he asked.

Elizabeth gawked at the man in black as if she couldn't believe her eyes. "You didn't let them kill me!" she blurted.

Preacher moved to the swinging doors and peered out.

The youngest Bascomb was sprawled on his back a few feet from the doorway.

There was no sign of Ira and Boone.

Preacher took Elizabeth's right hand. "We must leave. I have a horse behind the livery. If we can reach him, I'll have you safe with your father by morning."

"I'm ready," Elizabeth told him.

Someone moaned.

"Did you hear that?" Elizabeth inquired.

Preacher looked at the bar. The sound had issued from behind it. He crouched and approached the north end of the bar, at a loss to explain the moan. As he reached the bar, the person moaned again.

"Will!" Elizabeth cried, and raced past Preacher. She ran behind the bar, then ducked from sight.

Preacher gazed over the counter. Despite the darkness, he recognized the figure of Lieutenant James.

Elizabeth was on her knees, cradling the lieutenant's head in her lap. "Will!" she exclaimed happily. "You're alive! You're alive!"

Lieutenant James opened his eyes. He grinned at Elizabeth and tried to speak, but couldn't.

Eliabeth glanced up at the man in black. "We can't leave now!"

"The Bascombs are lurking outside somewhere," Preacher reminded her.

"I don't care," Elizabeth said. "I'm not leaving Will!"

Preacher pondered his next move. "There was a Crow with Lieutenant James," he mentioned. "What happened to him?"

Elizabeth's sadness was evident in her tone. "Lone Eagle was killed by Boone Bascomb."

Preacher had liked the old Indian. He frowned, thinking of someone else he'd liked—Brooke Merriweather. And Brooke, like his mother, his sister, Chelsea Glen, and Rosamond Langehorne, was dead. If he didn't know any better, Preacher told himself, he'd swear he was bad medicine for any woman in his life.

"What will you do?" Elizabeth inquired, rousing him from his reflection.

"I'll tend to the Bascombs," Preacher said. "You stay put! Don't even stick your nose from behind this bar! Stay here until you know it's over."

"How will I know that?" Elizabeth asked.

"You'll know," Preacher assured her. He started to run.

"Preacher!" Elizabeth called out.

"What?"

"Don't get yourself killed!" Elizabeth declared. "Please!" she added softly. "I don't want another life on my hands!"

"I aim to stay alive," Preacher assured her. He hurried to the ruined window and leaned against the jamb near the doorway.

Night still ruled Ten Sleep. Bodies littered the street. Nothing else stirred.

Ira and Boone Bascomb were out there somewhere, Preacher knew, waiting for him to step into the street. They weren't about to hightail it out of Ten Sleep. Not now. They owed Preacher too much. They'd kill him, or perish in the attempt. But what tactics would they use? Call him out on the street? Not likely. They'd tried a standup fight once and it hadn't worked. Try to get to him through Elizabeth Demming? No.

Ira had lost his ace in the hole, and he undoubtedly wouldn't bother to try and recapture her until Preacher was disposed of. So it narrowed down to a test of nerves. Ira and Boone, waiting, guns ready, in hiding, expecting Preacher to come after them.

There was no sense in disappointing them.

Preacher replaced the used rounds in his hip gun. He glanced at the bar once, insuring Elizabeth and Lieutenant James were out of sight. Then he vaulted over the window sill and dashed into the street, hoping Ira and Boone would be concentrating on the swinging doors. They must have been. He was two-thirds of the way across when Boone's big gun blasted from the general direction of the livery. Something tugged at Preacher's hat, but he reached the front of the general store unscathed. So Boone was at the livery. But where was Ira?

Preacher moved toward the livery, passing the general store entrance. He was abreast of the front window in two more strides.

A loud crash erupted from inside.

Preacher threw himself to the plank walk, his arms outstretched, as two gunshots cracked from inside and the general store window dissolved in a shower of glass.

Ira was in the general store!

Preacher scurried to the far side of the window and rose to his knees. He peered inside.

A large shadowy figure was moving in the vicinity of the

counter.

Preacher fired once, and the figure dropped to the floor, sending a stack of cans tumbling.

Then silence.

Preacher stood, staying to the left of the window, and listened. he could hear the breeze, but that was it. No other sounds came from within the store. Had he hit Ira?

Something rustled inside.

The curtain? Was Ira crawling toward the storeroom? Preacher turned and darted into the alley, then raced to the rear of the general store. If Ira attempted to climb out the rear window, he'd be in for a surprise!

But the surprise was all Preacher's.

Boone Bascomb appeared at the end of the alley, his needle gun leveled.

Preacher lunged to the right as the Springfield .50-70 boomed, but too late. The slug dug a deep furrow in his left side below the ribs. He crouched, his finger on the trigger, but Boone had already ducked to safety.

The Bascombs were slipprier than a snake coated with bacon fat!

Preacher ran to the end of the alley.

Boone Bascomb was gone.

Preacher squatted against the rear wall of the general store, presenting as small a target as possible. This was getting him nowhere! The Bascombs could take pot shots at him all night, and sooner or later their aim would be equal to the occasion. Instead of traipsing willy-nilly all over Ten Sleep, he had to flush the bastards into the open, force them to come after him, conduct the fight on his terms, not theirs.

Walking down the middle of the main street, calling their name, would do the trick, but it would also get him killed. No. Preacher needed to lure them from hiding. An idea occurred to him, and he grinned as he rose and ran down the alley. He took a right when he reached the main street, and there was his destination forty yards off—the livery.

They had to have their horses somewhere.

Preacher's legs pumped as he sprinted the remaining distance and reached the large livery doors. He looked behind him. The main street was seemingly deserted. He threw the right hand door open.

Five horses occupied stalls inside.

Preacher stepped inside and pulled the door in, leaving it ajar. He ran to the rear of the livery and exited through the back door.

His stallion was tethered in the spot where he'd left him.

Preacher slid his hip gun into its scabbard. He walked up to his horse and reached into his bedroll. His right hand closed on the .58 caliber and he withdrew it. The stock was already attached, and the pistol-carbine was loaded with seven cartridges.

Time to put his plan into action.

Preacher reentered the livery and crossed to the front doors. He peered out, studying the street. Not a flicker of life anywhere. He shoved the door wide open, then walked to the nearest stall.

What would Ira and Boone do, he wondered, if their horses suddenly hit the breeze without them?

Preacher started the first animal toward the open door. He slapped it on the thigh. "Get out of here!"

The horse shied, trotted through the open door and then galloped to the west.

Preacher repeated the procedure with another animal. He watched the horse disappear into the night, then turned and scanned the main street.

Movement.

The Bascombs had taken notice of the departure of their mounts. Both were advancing toward the livery, coming from the general store and staying in the deeper blackness near the buildings they passed.

Preacher hurried to the first empty stall. A saddle was on a rail to his right. He grabbed it by the horn and deposited it in the center of the stall. He quickly did the same with all the saddles he could find, stacking them, constructing a mound behind which a man might hide. Then he moved to the occupied stall directly across from the stall containing the saddles. A skittish black stallion eyed him warily as he angled into the stall alongside it.

Outside the front door, something crunched.

Preacher crouched. A chink in the stall enabled him to see the front doors.

A minute passed.

Two.

A hand appeared, gripping the edge of the right hand door.

The door was slowly eased outward.

Something scraped near the rear door.

Preacher glanced over his shoulder. The back door was not visible from the stall. He figured one of the Bascombs had snuck around to the rear of the livery. They intended to come at him from both directions simultaneously. Pretty slick, but predictable.

Ira Bascomb's bushy face popped out from behind the front door. He scrutinized the interior of the livery, stall by stall, seeking Preacher. Then he glanced toward the back of the livery and shook his head.

Preacher's grip on the .58 tightened.

Ira eased around the door, stealthily creeping into the livery, the Remington New Model Army .44 in his right hand. An Arkansas toothpick was strapped to his right hip.

Preacher placed his finger on the trigger of the .58.

Ira advanced, looking to the left and the right, his eyes never still. He was convinced it was a trap. But they couldn't allow Preacher to spook their horses. A man afoot was in serious trouble on the prairie, particularly if the army was on his trail.

The black stallion abruptly whinnied.

Ira stared at the stallion's stall.

Preacher tensed.

Ira watched the black stallion for a moment longer, then proceeded. The barrel of the Remington swept from side to side.

A foot padded to Preacher's left.

Boone Bascomb, his needle gun held at waist level, appeared at the end of the stall. He reached out and stroked the stallion's cheek.

Ira made a nodding motion with his head, indicating the stall with the stacked saddles.

Boone and Ira converged on the stall, hardware at the ready, and pointed at the pile of saddles.

Preacher slowly rose, but stayed hunched over. He took a step toward the aisle.

Boone hesitated, staring at his father questioningly.

Ira impatiently motioned with his Remington for Boone to keep going.

Preacher took another step.

The Bascombs, one on either side of the opposite stall,

# SLAUGHTER AT TEN SLEEP

were three yards from their goal.

Preacher crept around the black stallion.

The Bascombs were obviously confused. The stack of saddles *looked* like a hiding place. But they couldn't be certain, because the inside of the livery was gloomy and dark. Outside, the storm clouds had parted, allowing a sliver of moon to illuminate the landscape. But insufficient light penetrated into the center of the livery.

Boone leaned forward. "Hell!" he declared. "He ain't in here!"

"Wrong, knothead!" Preacher stated harshly.

The Bascombs, startled, recovered instantly, spinning to confront their enemy.

Preacher shot Ira first, the .58 thundering and slamming the giant against the far stall.

Boone's needle gun was sweeping around, the barrel almost pointed at the Widow Maker's chest.

Preacher fired, the .58 bucking in his hands.

Boone Bascomb was smashed to the floor by the impact. He landed on his back, still attempting to elevate the Springfield's barrel.

Preacher shot Boone again, in the chest, and Boone was flipped onto his left side, his back to Preacher.

Preacher gazed at the bodies and nodded. The Bascombs were finished! Or were they?

Incredibly, Boone Bascomb suddenly rolled over, raising his needle gun for one more try.

Preacher moved closer. He aimed the .58 at the middle of Boone's face and squeezed the trigger.

Boone gasped as he was propelled three feet along the floor to crash into the far stall. The Springfield fell from his fingers. He uttered a sucking noise, then was still.

Preacher walked up to Boone. He leaned over, examining Boone's face, insuring he was dead. There was no doubt about it. A substantial portion of Boone's face was missing.

*Now* it was over.

Preacher sighed as he wearily walked to the livery doors. Most of his fights were over in the blink of an eye. When shootists took to settling disputes by throwing down on one another, the affair was concluded in the instant of time it took the winner to draw and fire. But this had been different. A grueling, protracted affair. He'd definitely earned the five-thousand dollars General Demming had offered. Every penny of it.

A cool breeze was blowing from the northwest.

Preacher turned toward the saloon. His left side was hurting terribly. The .50-70 must have dug a gash six inches long and an inch deep. He felt a sticky substance clinging to his shirt, and realized he'd been bleeding the whole time. Blood loss could be critical without a doctor in attendance.

Isolated clouds were swirling across the sky.

Preacher reached the walk in front of the saloon. He was about to push open the swinging doors when a female voice stopped him cold.

"Freeze! Or I'll shoot!"

"Elizabeth!" Preacher said. "I'm too tired to fight you, too!"

"Preacher? Is that you?"

Preacher walked into the saloon. "I thought I told you to stay put!"

Elizabeth came around the north end of the bar. Lieutenant James' sidearm was in her right hand. "I'm sorry. I mistook you for one of the Bascombs."

"There are no more Bascombs," Preacher informed her.

"Ira and Boone are dead?" Elizabeth asked hopefully.

"As dead as a person can get," Preacher confirmed. "How is Lieutenant James?"

"He's asleep," Elizabeth said. "He needs a doctor."

"He's not the only one," Preacher stated. "Can you find a match and light one of the lanterns?"

"I know where the matches are," Elizabeth replied. She groped along the bar counter. "Here! I found them!" She moved to a nearby table, and within moments the saloon was bathed in a yellowish glow. She looked at the man in black. "You look terrible!" she commented.

"Thanks," Preacher responded. He sat on one of the tables, depositing the .58 next to his right leg.

"Were you hit?" Elizabeth inquired, coming forward.

"Afraid so," Preacher answered, gritting his teeth. He slowly unbuttoned his white shirt and inched his right hand inside.

"Is it bad?" Elizabeth asked.

"Don't know yet," Preacher said.

His probing fingers touched the wound, tracing its dimensions. He'd underestimated its size; the laceration was more like seven inches in length. When he pulled his hand from under the shirt, his fingers were dripping with blood.

"Dear Lord!" Elizabeth exclaimed in alarm. "You need tending."

"It will need to wait," Preacher remarked. "We must get you to your father."

"There's no hurry," Elizabeth said. "The Bascombs are all dead."

"Not yet, they ain't!" growled a guttural voice from the doorway.

Preacher grabbed for the .58.

A gun cracked, and a slug tore into the table near Preacher's hand.

"Try that again, Preacher, and I'll perforate your head!"

Ira Bascomb stood in the doorway, his Remington in his right hand. The entire right side of his brown shirt was stained with crimson.

"No!" Elizabeth cried, staring at the patriarch in horrified fascination.

"Yes!" Ira retorted. He strode into the saloon, the Remington barrel trained on Preacher's head. "We nicked you, did we?" he said, nodding at Preacher's left side.

Preacher nodded. "I figured you for dead."

"You figured wrong," Ira rejoined. "Now I want you to unlimber your artillery. Real careful like."

Preacher used his thumb and first finger to draw his hip gun.

"Set it on the floor," Ira directed.

Preacher complied.

"I know you tote a vest gun," Ira said. "On the floor with it."

Preacher eased his frock coat inside, displaying the vest gun. He removed the forty-four forty and placed in next to it mate.

Ira visibly relaxed, even grinned. "Now we can tend to business."

Preacher was surprised by Ira's calm attitude. He leaned back on the table, propping his body with his hands, putting his hands that much nearer to the Bowie cradled in the small of his back.

Ira suddenly pressed his right hand to his mouth and

coughed. The Remington never wavered. He finished coughing and lowered his hand, revealing a trickle of blood flowing from the left corner of his mouth.

"You won't last long," Preacher commented.

"Neither will you, you son of a bitch!" Ira snapped. He glowered at the man in black and the general's daughter. "I could've shot you dead before you even knew I was here," he boasted. "But I didn't. Don't you want to know why?"

"I have a feeling you'll tell us," Preacher said.

Ira glared at the Widow Maker. "Cutting you down would be too easy! I want you to suffer! I want you to pay for what you did to my boys! They're all dead! Every single one of 'em!" Ira's features were distorted by his fury. "I want you to pay, Preacher! I want you to suffer! I want you to die, slow, so I can watch you! You savvy, Widow Maker?"

Preacher didn't bother to respond.

Ira drew his Arkansas toothpick. Like the Bowie, the Arkansas toothpick was a large sheath knife. But the Arkansas toothpick was slimmer, not quite as heavy or as long as the Bowie. "I aim to whittle you down to size!" Ira vowed.

Preacher was sorely tempted to draw his Bowie, but he decided to bide his time. That Remington barrel was centered on his forehead.

Ira took several steps toward Preacher. He chuckled and waved his knife blade in the air. "You'll be beggin' for mercy by the time I'm done with you!"

"I wouldn't count on it," Preacher mocked him.

Ira looked at Elizabeth. "But what am I to do about you while I'm havin' my fun?"

"My father will see you hang!" Elizabeth said bitterly.

"We all die, one way or another," Ira stated. He scanned the saloon. "Frankly, Miss Demming, I don't much care how or when I bite the dust. All my boys are gone. I've nothin' left to live for, except," he grinned at Preacher, "killin' you!"

"You don't care about the gold any more?" Preacher asked.

Ira pursed his lips, then shook his head. "No. Can't say as I do. Sort of funny, ain't it? I come this far on account of the damn gold! Now all my boys are kilt! And I don't give a hoot 'bout the lousy gold!"

"Then let the girl go," Preacher said.

"What?"

"Why not?" Preacher queried. "You don't need her if you don't care about the gold. Let her ride out of Ten Sleep. Then you and I can settle up."

Ira stared at Elizabeth Demming. He saw her torn, dirty dress, her mud spattered shoes, her hair caked to her head, and the smudges on her face. "Git!" he told her.

"No."

Both Preacher and Ira faced her.

"What?" Ira asked.

"I won't leave!" Elizabeth insisted.

Preacher frowned. "Ride out while you have the chance," he advised. "Head east. You'll find Ten Sleep Canyon without any trouble. Your father is there."

Elizabeth shook her head. "I won't leave, and that's that!"

Ira chuckled. "You've got a heap of spunk for such a little filly!"

"You can find the doctor you wanted," Preacher said.

"What's she need a doc for?" Ira asked.

Elizabeth glanced at the bar, then at the doorway.

"The sooner you leave," Preacher prompted her, "the sooner the doctor will get here."

"What's she need a doc for?" Ira repeated.

He looked at Elizabeth. "If it's for Preacher, you might as well forget about it. He'll be dead by the time you make it back."

Elizabeth glanced at Preacher. She wasn't about to inform Ira about Lieutenant James. And she was grateful to Preacher for suggesting a means of possibly saving the officer she cared about.

"I'll do it," she declared.

"Take my horse," Preacher instructed her. "He's behind the livery, saddled and ready."

"I'll take good care of him," Elizabeth said. She headed for the doorway, then paused to stare into Preacher's eyes. "All those stories I heard about you and read about you, I know now they were a pack of lies. You're a much better man than they give you credit for being."

Ira snorted derisively.

Elizabeth whirled and dashed from the saloon.

"Ain't she sweet!" Ira said, chuckling. "I almost feel sorry 'bout kidnappin' her."

"Almost," Preacher noted.

Ira's features hardened. "If I was as bad as all that, I would have back shot you when I had the chance, wouldn't I?"

"I reckon," Preacher grudgingly admitted.

"We're more alike than you're willin' to admit," Ira said.

"What could we possibly have in common?" Preacher asked.

"We both believe in givin' the other feller an even break," Ira stated. " We believe in fightin' fair."

Preacher studied Ira Bascomb in a new light. Ira didn't seem quite as bloodthirsty, as ruthless. He even seemed to have an abiding sense of fairness.

Preacher looked into Ira's deep set eyes. "What about earlier? When you threatened to shoot Elizabeth?"

"I'd have never hurt her," Ira declared indignantly. "I wanted her to scream some, to draw you out."

Preacher nodded. He played poker, and he could appreciate a crafty bluff.

"Well, now that we're done chawin'," Ira said, "let's tend to business." He turned and tossed the Remington out the window.

Preacher's surprise showed.

Ira raised the Arkansas toothpick. "I told you I want you dead, Preacher. For killin' my brother Andy, and my boys. I'm goin' to hack you to pieces. But we'll do it fair and square. Let's see that pigsticker of yours."

Preacher eased to the floor. "You knew?"

"I'm not no greenhorn!" Ira replied.

Preacher reached behind his back and took hold of the Bowie with his right hand. He brought the big knife around.

Ira whistled in appreciation. "A Bowie! Always did like 'em. But this toothpick was a gift from my Pa." He crouched and transferred the knife from his left hand to his right.

Preacher extended the Bowie and bent at the waist, a posture intended to keep his abdomen and vital organs as far from Ira's knife point as possible.

"Prepare to meet your Maker!" Ira said. He laughed and charged.

Preacher back pedaled, avoiding the sweeping slashes of Ira's gleaming Arkansas toothpick. Preacher's knife was larger, but any advantage in knife size was more than offset by Ira's greater reach.

The giant chortled as he swung his knife, again and again and again, driving the man in black backwards, toward the bar.

Preacher blocked a wicked swipe at his privates, then took another step backwards. His spine collided with the bar. He couldn't retreat any further!

Ira grinned and lunged, aiming at Preacher's neck.

Preacher dodged to the left, narrowly avoiding the slashing knife.

The Arkansas toothpick slammed into the top of the bar, the point penetrating the wood and sticking fast.

Preacher closed, slicing his Bowie up and in, going for Ira's neck.

Ira was quicker. He released the toothpick and savagely backhanded the man in black across the face, sending him hurtling into a table.

Preacher felt the edge of the table dig into his injured left side, and then he was tumbling head over heels to the floor. He landed on his back, dazed.

Ira loomed above the upturned table, knife in hand.

Preacher rolled to his left as the toothpick descended, and the keen point just missed his legs. He bounded to his feet and turned.

Ira slammed into the man in black, wrapping his steely arms around the Widow Maker's legs and bearing him to the hardwood floor.

Preacher's head struck the floor with resounding force. He saw the room spin, and Ira's left hand clamped on his throat.

"Now!" Ira gloated. "This is for Andy!"

Preacher tried to squirm aside, but he couldn't escape the blow. He felt the toothpick imbed itself in his right shoulder, and he resisted an impulse to scream.

Ira jerked the knife free and raised it overhead. "And this is for Sherm!"

Preacher's right arm was useless, too numb to even hold the Bowie. He was completely at Ira's mercy, unless he did something fast. His speed and years of surviving by his wits served him in good stead. Even as the Arkansas toothpick started down, he whipped his left hand up and gouged his fingers into the giant's eyes.

The toothpick missed, smacking into the floor next to Preacher's left ear.

Ira bellowed and raised his left hand to his face.

Preacher bucked and heaved, dislodging his foe, sending Ira toppling to the side. He scrambled to his feet, taking the Bowie in his left hand.

Ira was erect, too, his eyes streaming tears. "Damn! You near blinded me!" he roared, and renewed his assault.

Preacher was compelled to retreat toward the front of the saloon, parrying blow after blow, their blades clanging as they clashed. Blood poured from Preacher's right shoulder. Ira's superior strength was slowly but surely wearing Preacher down.

Ira smirked, knowing he had the upper hand.

Preacher's left arm started to feel the strain. His muscles ached, his reflexes were slowing. He blocked a blow aimed at his face.

Ira unexpectedly stopped. "How you holdin' up, Preacher?" he sarcastically ridiculed the man in black. "You don't look too good. Maybe the general's girl had the right idea after all. Maybe you should see a doctor!" He laughed at his own joke.

Preacher shook his head to clear his sluggish senses. His right side was drenched in red, his right arm totally useless. Or was it? He tried to clench his fingers, succeeded.

"I'm enjoyin' this, Preacher!" Ira gloated.

A mad scheme took root in Preacher's mind.

"What part of you should I hack off first?" Ira asked gleefully. "An ear? Your nose? How 'bout one of your oysters?"

Preacher raised his left hand, the Bowie pointed upward.

"You in a hurry to die?" Ira demanded, then lunged.

Preacher fended off several swipes of the Arkansas toothpick, constantly backing off.

Ira beamed. He was deliberately driving the bounty hunter toward the shattered window, raining blow after blow, applying so much pressure Preacher was unable to properly concentrate. Which was exactly what Ira wanted.

The first intimation Preacher had he was in trouble came when his left boot heel bumped against the strip of wall below the window, and his knees caught on the lower sill.

Ira aimed a vicious swipe at Preacher's stomach.

Preacher had nowhere to go. He leaned back to evade the toothpick and lost his balance. For a moment he teetered on the edge of the sill, his left arm waving wildly, and then he fell backwards out the window.

Ira laughed.

Preacher rolled as he landed, twisting sideways, exposing his right side to the window and Ira, his supposedly useless side. He held his left hand behind his buttocks, then swiftly reversed his grip on the Bowie from the hilt to the blade. The hilt was now angled toward his right side. He rose to his knees.

Ira stepped up to the window sill. He leered down at Preacher, his face creased by a triumphant smile. "This is it, Widow Maker! The end of the line! You won't be makin' any more widows!" He paused, nodding appreciatively. "You put up a good fight, mister. The best I've ever seen. But it's over. Say your prayers."

Preacher was hunched over on his knees. He didn't comment.

"Nothin' to say, huh?" Ira asked. "Well, if that's the way you want it."

So saying, Ira stepped over the sill, his eyes on Preacher's left side, on his left shoulder, because Ira knew Preacher's right arm was worthless, rendered immobile by the damage caused by Preacher's right shoulder. Ira was confident of victory. There was no way Preacher could reach him with the Bowie, because Ira would see Preacher's left shoulder move as Preacher started his swing and sidestep the blow. Ira had it all figured out.

Almost.

Preacher knew Ira believed his right arm was incapable of movement. He knew Ira would be concentrating on his left arm. He knew the last thing Ira would expect would be for Preacher to use his right arm. So Preacher did. His right hand clasped the Bowie.

Ira was in midstride over the window sill when he saw Preacher's left shoulder flex and Preacher's left arm begin to sweep around. Focused as he was on the left arm, he failed to see the right arm driving up and in, failed to see the Bowie until it was too late. He did detect a motion out of the corner of his eye, but by then the Bowie's huge blade had speared into his testicles, shorn his balls right in half, and

Ira grunted as much from the pain as amazement. He stumbled and doubled over, his brawny hands reaching for his privates.

Preacher wrenched the Bowie free.

Ira shrieked.

Preacher's right hand was caked with Ira's blood, making the Bowie slippery to hold. But Preacher held on, pushing himself up with his left arm, ramming the Bowie straight in, burying the knife to the hilt in Ira Bascomb's throat.

Ira stiffened and gurgled, blood gushing from his mouth and neck. He dropped the Arkansas toothpick and clutched at his throat.

Preacher released the Bowie and staggered backwards, into the muddy street.

Ira futilely attempted to yank the Bowie from his neck. The geyser of blood poured over his hands and arms. He fixed incredulous eyes on Preacher and opened his mouth as if to speak. Instead, his eyes rolled in their sockets and he fell forward, his towering bulk crashing to the ground and spraying drops of blood in every direction.

Preacher stared at the body, half expecting it to rise again. His legs felt like mush, and he couldn't seem to stand still. He weaved and tottered, striving to return to the saloon. His feet had other ideas. They became entangled in something, and Preacher pitched to the ground, feeling the clammy mud on his cheeks and chin and hands. He tried to rise, and his consciousness faded.

# Epilogue

Preacher opened his eyes and the world came into sharp focus. He stared at his surroundings, puzzled. What had happened? He was in a warm bed, covered with quilts, his head resting on a comfortable pillow. The last thing he recalled was Ira Bascomb. How had he . . .

A door at the far end of the bedroom opened, and in walked Elizabeth Demming. She wore a bright blue dress and was carrying some sheets. Her eyes sparkled when she saw him. "Preacher! At last!" She ran to the side of the bed and took his right hand.

"Where am I?" Preacher croaked, his mouth and throat exceptionally dry.

"Hold your britches on," Elizabeth said. She moved to a small table and poured water into a glass from a pitcher. "Here," she declared, bearing the glass to the bed. "Drink this."

Preacher used his left hand to down the water. "Thanks," he said when finished.

"How do you feel?" Elizabeth asked.

"Tired," Preacher admitted. "And sore."

"The doctor said to expect that," Elizabeth informed him.

"Doctor?"

Elizabeth sat down on the edge of the bed. "You hush up. I don't think you should do much talking in your condition.

I'll go fetch Dr. Miller, but first I'd better tell you what happened before you burst at the seams."

She grinned. "You're at Fort Laramie, in our house. Father had you brought here from Ten Sleep. No one knows you are here. Father thought you might prefer it that way." She paused. "That horse of yours can fly like the wind! I found my father just like you said I would. We rode to Ten Sleep immediately, although he wanted me to rest. The dear!" Elizabeth smiled.

"What—" Preacher started to speak.

"I told you! No talking!" Elizabeth cut him off. "Here. This might explain a lot." She bent over and retrieved something from the floor. "You read this while I go for Dr. Miller and my father."

It was an edition to the Rocky Mountain News. Five days old.

Five days! Had he been unconscious that long? Preacher opened the paper, scarcely aware when Elizabeth departed. He found the story he wanted on page three.

### SLAUGHTER AT TEN SLEEP

The U.S. Army has declared martial law in this normally quiet settlement located in the Wyoming Territory. A band of ruffians, an outlaw clan whose leader once rode with the infamous William Quantrill, raided this community and sent its residents fleeing in the night. A pair of prominent citizens were killed by the outlaws. They have been identified as Colin Rennert, owner of the Tiger Saloon, and Brooke Merriweather, owner of the general store.

The Army sent troops in to quell the disturbance. Five members of the outlaw clan, all named Bascomb, were killed in the battle which ensued. Before they succumbed, the Bascombs took the lives of ten valiant soldiers and one Indian scout. Another soldier, identified as Lieutenant William James, was seriously injured. He is being rushed to Fort Laramie for medical treatment.

The news has learned these same Bascombs

were responsible for kidnapping the daughter of General Nels Demming. She was rescued unharmed.

The Army has done peace loving citizens everywhere a service by exterminating yet another band of lawless villains, whose breed, unfortunately, has flourished since the end of the War.

Preacher lowered the paper. General Nels Demming had covered his tracks, a wise move considering the uproar the story would create if the headline-hungry journalists ever learned the Widow Maker was involved. He stared up at the white ceiling, reflecting. The general had brought him into the Demming home, so the general was unquestionably grateful to Preacher for saving his daughter. But how thankful would the general be, Preacher wondered, if Demming knew it was him, and not the Bascombs, who was responsible for killing the ten dead soldiers? Not very grateful, Preacher realized. And only a complete fool would disclose the truth.

Preacher was no fool.

The bedroom door opened and Elizabeth entered, out of breath. "I sent word to my father and Dr. Miller," she said as she came toward the bed. "They should be here directly."

"Lieutentant James . . . ?" Preacher inquired.

Elizabeth grinned from ear to ear. "He's downstairs in another bedroom. Dr. Miller says it might take up to six months for Will to mend. I can't wait for him to get back on his feet!"

Preacher's mouth twisted upward in one of his rare, genuine smiles.

Elizabeth turned to leave. "I'll go watch for Dr. Miller." She took several steps, then stopped. "Oh! Before I forget! Your horse is being taken care of, and your gear is under your bed."

"Thanks," Preacher said, and he meant it.

Elizabeth reached the door and looked back, grinning impishly. "One more thing . . ."

"What?" Preacher asked.

"I know how you shootists need to practice a lot,"

Elizabeth said, "but I'll thank you not to use our fixtures for targets. Besides, you might accidentally hit Will." She winked, giggled and left.

J. D. Preacher, for the first time in ages, laughed.

Preacher rode east from Fort Laramie on September 3, 1869. His body had healed rapidly, and he'd worked the lingering stiffness out of his right side using daily exercise and constant practice with his forty-four forties. He carried with him five-thousand dollars, and the heartfelt appreciation of three new friends, genuine friends, the kind a man in his profession seldom acquired while enforcing Preacher's Law.

The man in black rode into the sunrise of a new day.